# Over the Water and Into the Woods

## Barrie Day

Created via the KDP Publishing Platform

Distribution via
Bookcase
19, Castle St,
Carlisle. CA3 8SY

ISBN 978-1912181-60-5
First Printed 2023

Most of the illustrations, including the book
cover, are adapted from original photographs
taken by the author.

## DEDICATION

To
my wife Sue
and
our five wonderful grandchildren
who were the inspiration
for this book


## ACKNOWLEDGEMENT

Thanks, as always, to Sue
for her diligent proof reading, and her
insights and sound judgement
regarding the style and content
of the book

# INTRODUCING

Mason    Harry    Max  Charlie  Summer

Sophya

# Where it all happened

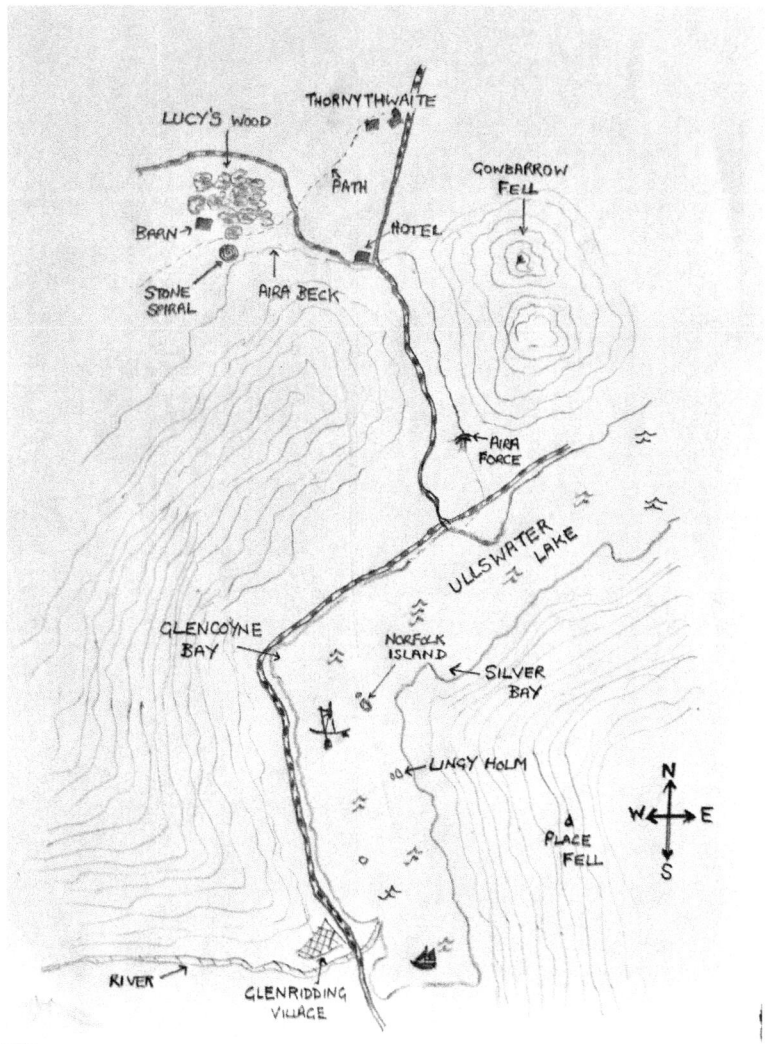

Southern end of Ullswater Lake

## CHAPTER 1

So there it was - her foot was stuck, well and truly stuck! And she'd chosen this particular tree because it had a good view down the road. What she hadn't noticed was the small gap where the main trunk branched so when she pushed down to get higher up the tree her trainer had lodged tight between the two branches. She wriggled her toes, tried to bend her ankle but it was no good. Her foot was stuck!

Summer had wanted to be the first to see the cousins' car come round the bend in the road, then the holiday could really start. She loved being with Harry and Charlie - they were fun. Not that her own brothers, Mason and Max, couldn't also be fun but often Mason had his head in a book and Max was usually lost in a world of Lego armies or glued to his screen playing another football game.

What to do? She didn't want to call for help - the boys would really tease her then. Her parents were busy unpacking inside the cottage and probably wouldn't hear her. Below, Kip, the border collie, stood looking up at her. Maybe Kip could help? The one thing Summer really loved was dogs. And the minute she spotted Kip when they drove into the farmyard at Thornythwaite Farm she knew this was going to be a great holiday. Kip had bounded up to them and dropped a stick at Summer's feet. Then he backed away, looking first at the stick and then at Summer. It was obvious what he wanted.

She had thrown the stick and Kip had chased after it. It landed in some long grass but Kip soon found it. He was back within minutes, dropping the stick again and looking up at Summer with his eyes bright, ears pricked, tail wagging.

'Can you help me, Kip?' muttered Summer, more to herself than the dog. 'I don't want Harry and Charlie to arrive and find me stuck in a tree. How dumb would that look!'

Near her left hand she saw a dead branch. She broke off a piece and held it up for Kip.

'Look Kip, stick! Stick!' She pretended to throw it and the dog made a quick movement to go after it. But then he came back to the base of the tree and stood looking up, waiting. If she could get him barking, maybe that would attract attention and she wouldn't have to call for help. She pretended to throw the stick again, Kip was about to chase after it then realised he was being fooled, so he barked with frustration.

'That's it, Kip, keep barking,' said Summer. She waved the stick again and now Kip realised this was some sort of game. He barked again. Then he kept barking.

It was Max who appeared first. He saw his sister up the tree. 'What's wrong with Kip and what are you doing up there?'

'Oh, I was just looking out for Harry and Charlie.'

'I found a great place to build a den,' said Max. 'Just up the hillside there's a fallen tree and underneath there's a big space where you can crawl in.'

Summer didn't mention how long she'd been stuck. She just said casually. 'Give my foot a push up, can you Max, it seems to have got kind of wedged.'

Max climbed on to a lower branch, reached up and pushed the sole of Summer's shoe out of the cleft in the tree. Summer breathed a sigh of relief just as a grey car came down the road and turned into the farmyard. The cousins had arrived!

Charlie was wearing a Manchester United shirt and Harry wore a Liverpool top. The one had 'Chazmo' written across the back and Harry's said 'Hazmo'.

'When did you get the new tops?' asked Max.

Harry pointed at Charlie. 'It was when ManU got battered by Newcastle. Charlie was down in the dumps.'

'Not true,' retorted Charlie. 'It was when I won that bet that Liverpool would get smashed by Everton. And they did!'

Max nodded. This was the usual banter between the twins. Harry and Charlie generally got on quite well except when it came to football.

'Hey, what a cool place,' said Charlie looking at the cottages. They were converted farm buildings built of solid blocks of Lakeland stone, curving in an L-shape round a cobbled yard.

'Did you see the lake?' asked Max. 'We saw loads of people on paddleboards and sailboats.'

'Yes, we drove along the edge of it. Ullswater, I think it's called,' replied Harry. 'We brought our canoe and paddle board.'

'There were a couple of islands in the lake,' added Charlie. 'We thought we could paddle out to explore them.'

'And there's some mega waterfall just above the lake. Dad said we'll be hiking to it,' said Max.

'And Max found a place to build a den,' added Summer.

'Yes, there's loads of places to explore here,' said Max. 'It's going to be fun!'

Just then, Mason emerged from a small coppice of trees behind the main farmhouse. He was whittling a point on a small length of wood. He had a pair of binoculars slung round his neck.

'Where've you been?' asked Charlie.

'Just trying out this new penknife. Got it last birthday, but I've never really used it. It's brilliant for sharpening sticks and there's so much wood lying around. And from the hill back there you can just start to see the lake. What a great place this is.'

The farmhouse and cottages were owned by Victoria and Jim, friends of Mason's grandparents. Their son Thomas had a large flock of sheep which were grazing in the surrounding fields. It was lambing time and Thomas was busy working long days, late nights and early mornings checking on his ewes, making sure they were birthing their lambs successfully.

'Victoria said that if we're up early we might see some lambs being born,' said Summer excitedly.

Charlie grimaced. 'Not sure I could stomach that before breakfast.'

'We watched lambing on tele last week,' added Harry. 'Lots of slime and blood. Pretty gross at times, I can tell you.'

But Summer was not to be put off. 'Well I don't care, I'm going to be up early to see what happens.'

CHAPTER 2

The following morning Summer and Max were up before the others had stirred. The morning air was chilly, the sun just striking the edges of the eastern fells and Max shivered as he and Summer made their way across the farmyard to the barn where Thomas was kneeling next to a ewe. The sheep was panting and Thomas was resting his hand on its belly, pressing gently.

Victoria was there leaning over the small pen where the ewe was due to give birth. She pointed. 'Thomas is just feeling to check the position of the lamb, whether it's in the correct position for a smooth birth. In a minute he's going to feel inside the mother and try to ease out the lamb.'

Summer and Max watched open-mouthed as Thomas slid his hand inside the rear end of the sheep. He found the small front legs of the lamb, pulled and within a matter of seconds the slimy, bloodied legs, head and body of the little lamb slithered out onto the straw of the pen.

Summer put her hand to her mouth and gasped. Max glanced at her and put his hand on his little sister's arm. Even his stomach felt a bit queasy at what they were seeing.

Thomas shook the limp body, wiped the mucus from its nostrils, lifted it and placed it close to the mother's panting mouth. The lamb's body twitched a couple of times, then the mother started licking the red slime from the coat of the lamb and soon the little creature was struggling onto its quivering legs.

'That little fella is going to be fine,' nodded Victoria. 'We were a bit worried about this ewe, that's why she's been brought into the barn.'

'What are you doing now?' asked Max, as he watched Thomas go back to the rear end of the ewe.

'There's probably at least one more, if not two,' replied Thomas. 'She was pretty big, this one, and she was really struggling out in the field.'

Sure enough another lamb was eased out from the ewe by Thomas pulling firmly on the two front legs. This lamb was bigger but like the other one, it was soon being licked clean by the mother.

The first lamb gave a pitiful bleat and Summer shook her head and smiled. 'He's going to be okay. I was a bit worried for a minute.'

'They're tougher than you think,' said Victoria.

*

After breakfast that first morning they did a hike across the valley and followed the Aira Beck down to the dramatic waterfall, Aira Force. At first, the path ran along the foot of Gowbarrow Fell before it left the open meadow and dropped into woodland and followed closer to the river. Charlie led the way, slashing at nettles and brambles with a stick he'd been working on using Mason's knife. The stick had a fork at the handle end. He'd seen the one that Thomas carried with him. Thomas called it a 'thumb stick' and said that farmers and shepherds carried them for prodding sheep, keeping frisky cattle at bay, or for leaning on when you were checking over a flock of sheep. Charlie had trimmed off the side branches, smoothed the surface by whittling the rough bark and shaved the handle end so that his thumb sat

comfortably in the curve of the fork. Max liked the look of Charlie's thumb stick so planned to make one for himself when they got back to the farm.

The river gradient steepened and now the water flowed fast over boulders, plunged through narrow gullies and gorges and bubbled into deep pools. The water was crystal clear and the sun was lighting up the bands of colour in the rock strata and glinting off the smooth stones in the base of the pool.

Harry and Mason slithered down the river bank above one of these pools and were challenging each other to jump in. But a clear shake of the head from Harry's father put an end to that idea.

They began to hear a dull roar ahead of them. The river was noisy with the gushing and hiss of the spume against the rocks, but this was a different sound - deep and hollowed out. They'd reached Aira Force.

There was a small bridge over the main waterfall which plunged from a narrow gorge into a wide pool twenty metres below. The sides of the gorge were damp with a covering of dark green moss, the air was moist and cold and here the sun didn't penetrate the shade.

'This is like a place of witches and wizards,' remarked Charlie.

'I think it's spooky,' added Summer, as she watched the ribbons of water dribbling down the walls of the gorge.

'Tricky building this bridge,' commented Mason. 'Says on this sign that it was built early in the 20th century. Wonder how they supported the bridge while they were building it.'

'Probably turned off the waterfall while they were working on it,' said Harry.

'What d'you mean?' asked Summer, frowning. She was puzzled by the idea of turning off a waterfall.

'He's just kidding,' grinned Charlie looking over the edge of the bridge. 'But it is pretty impressive.'

Summer shook her head. Her cousins were always kidding her about something and it was never easy to get her own back. One day maybe.

That evening the two families walked the half mile down to the Royal Hotel which stood

near the river in the village of Dockray. The hotel had a big garden at the front and on the lawn stood a huge chess board and a set of chess pieces, each one half as tall as Summer. While they were waiting for drinks to arrive they set up the chess pieces. Mason, Charlie and Harry had played chess a few times and reckoned they knew where the pieces should be placed on the chequered board.

'Pawns in the line at the front,' said Mason.

'Castles in the four corners,' added Charlie.

Harry shifted the white Queen into position. 'Queen on its own colour.'

'What's this one called?' asked Max, pushing a piece with a domed head across the board.

'That's the bishop,' replied Mason.

'And this is the knight,' said Harry pushing a piece with a horse's head next to the castle.

The adults sat down at one of the picnic tables as a waiter came across the grass with a tray of drinks.

Summer wasn't interested in the chess game so she wandered off to another part of the garden to look at some stone statues. It was then she had a curious feeling she was being watched. Where the feeling came from she wasn't sure but out of the corner of her eye she sensed a quick movement. She turned her head but there was nothing there. She moved on to examine another statue, glancing over her shoulder as she did so. This statue was a lady holding a bunch of grapes and looking upwards. Summer ran her hand over the smooth surface of the lady's shoulder.

Then another movement. She turned quickly and was in time to see a small blonde head wearing a baseball cap. From behind an old wooden barrel, two eyes were staring at her. The blonde hair was tied with a yellow and blue ribbon.

Just at that moment there was a shriek of 'Check' from one of the boys. Summer turned at the sound, then turned back but the person with the yellow and blue ribbon had gone. Summer went across to the wooden barrel and looked behind. Nothing there, just a path leading to a door into the hotel.

Later that evening when they had all finished their meal the boys went outside to finish off their chess game. Summer went off to find the toilet. It was as she was closing the door of the cubicle that she heard the main toilet door creaking open. There were light footsteps and then a small hand appeared under her cubicle door pushing a piece of folded paper. There was a silver ring on a finger of the hand and the nails were painted alternately light blue and yellow. The footsteps retreated, the main door creaked open and then closed with a soft hiss. Summer bent down and picked up the note. There was a single word written on it in red ink - HELP.

Maybe this was a game, thought Summer. She wasn't sure what to do so she put the piece of paper into the pocket of her jeans and decided to wait a while. She didn't want to be teased by the boys for being 'over dramatic' as Mason sometimes called her. 'You're being over dramatic,' he would say when she got upset or worried over something. It wasn't easy being the youngest with two older brothers. Max and Mason often called her 'pipsqueak' which made her sound a bit silly. Well she wasn't going to do anything now that might be seen as silly. She would keep the piece of paper to herself for a while. It was her secret.

## CHAPTER 3

'I need to tell you about Lucy's Wood,' said Victoria. She had arrived at the cottage door with a tray of new laid eggs. Breakfast was almost over and Victoria pulled a chair up to the table. 'You'll enjoy this walk, it's to a very special place which I think you'll love.'

'Who's Lucy?' asked Harry.

'Lucy Farncombe was the daughter of some neighbours of ours who live just up the valley. Tragically, Lucy died in 1996 when she was in her teens but before she died she asked her parents if they would plant a wood in her memory and make it a place not of sadness but a place which would lift people's spirits.'

'And did they do it?' asked Max. 'Did they plant a wood?'

Victoria nodded. 'They did and it's a beautiful wood with lots of paths winding through the trees. There are places to sit, some wonderful views but most of all there's a very special stone barn which is a place for some quiet thinking. There's always a candle burning there in memory of Lucy. It's called 'Lucy's Barn'. You'll see Lucy's name carved on a stone slab above the door.'

'How far is it?' asked Mason.

'Not far,' replied Victoria. 'The barn is on a hillside where there's a small stream which runs down through the wood to Aira Beck in the bottom of the valley. The beck has plunge pools and gorges where the river can be quite fierce so you have to be careful.'

'Sounds interesting,' nodded Charlie's mother, 'we'll get ourselves organised and go and check it out. Agreed?'

Everybody nodded.

Summer frowned. 'Shame about poor Lucy, though.'

'And she was so young,' added Harry. 'That's terrible.'

'It was ,' agreed Victoria. 'But I think you'll find that Lucy's Wood is not a place of sadness but a place of real joy. Anyway, when you get back, come and tell me what you think about the place. Okay?'

'We will,' replied Mason.

The path to Lucy's Wood followed the line of the dry stone wall which bordered the field behind the farmhouse. They set off with Max leading the way, slashing at nettles with the new thumb stick he'd been working on.

'Not quite finished yet,' he said when Charlie came for a closer look.

Charlie ran his finger and thumb over the handle and down the shaft of the stick. He nodded. 'Pretty good job, Max.'

'Thanks,' he said, pleased to get this nod of approval from his older cousin. 'Thomas said hazel was a good wood for a thumb stick and he showed me where to find some.'

Harry was at the back of the group scanning the sky with Mason's binoculars. He'd seen a falcon perched on a fence post earlier that morning  and now he'd spotted another bird of prey circling in spirals above Gowbarrow Fell. A buzzard, he reckoned, from the shape of the wings. He was hoping he might see a red kite, which he'd read about - a bird which had a very distinctive wedge-shaped tail and a curious gliding and swooping way of flying, but so far, no luck.

Summer, deep in thought, was walking with Mason. 'D'you think Lucy's ghost is in the wood? It sounds a bit scary to me.'

Mason put a reassuring hand on Summer's shoulder. 'Don't start getting worried. Victoria said it was a happy place. I think it sounds amazing to plant a wood for someone. It wasn't all that long ago so the trees will probably be quite small. Just keep close to me and you'll be fine.'

They crossed a lane and then the path sloped down a meadow towards some woods. They could hear the sound of rushing water and soon spotted a broad meander of Aira Beck down a sheer slope far below them.

Charlie peered down into the chasm. 'Wow, that's quite a drop. Good job there's a fence.'

They skirted the bend in the river and climbed out of the trees, up through another meadow and came to a gate in a wall.

'I think this is it,' said Charlie. 'There's a stone here with some writing on it.'

The letters were deeply etched into the slab of stone.

Max stooped down and ran his hand across the surface of the stone slab. 'It says Lucy's Wood.'

'There you are,' said Mason to Summer. 'I don't think it's going to be scary.'

There were clusters of small trees and, as they progressed further, the trees thickened. There were winding paths branching off deeper into the wood.

Summer felt a shiver like small fingers running down her back. So this was it. The wood they had planted for Lucy. She followed close behind Mason up another path which led into the wood. In the distance she could see the roof of a building. This must be the barn with the candle which was always burning. Another shiver.

'Wow!' shouted Harry, 'look at this stone. I like the way this one's carved.' He was stooping down examining a flat stone in the grass.

On it were carved the words:

*For everything*
*I feel a love,*
*the weeds below*
*the birds above.*

Summer ran her fingers over the letters. 'That's a nice thing to write,' she said.

Harry was scanning the hillside ahead of them. 'Look over there, there's a stream running down into some small ponds, the one feeds into the next. How clever is that!'

The stream emerged from the woods behind a stone building and ran down the hillside into one pond, which then cascaded into a second pond and then into a third before disappearing down the hillside in the direction of Aira Beck in the valley bottom.

Max was the first to reach the building but he hesitated before putting his hand on the latch of the heavy oak door. He decided to wait until the others arrived. Above the door was a carved stone which said: *Lucy 1978-'96*.

Lucy's Barn was a single storey building made from huge lumps of rock and river boulders. It was roofed with slabs of Lakeland slate. The building squatted snugly on the hillside sheltered by a steep rock cliff and a cluster of pine trees. From a branch of one of the trees hung a rope swing. Max chose the rope swing rather than opening the door.

The adults had been trailing behind on the walk but now Max's father arrived. He opened the door. 'Now remember, this is a special place. You need to stay quiet and spare a thought for Lucy.'

But Summer had not stopped thinking of Lucy and the blonde haired girl at the hotel and the piece of paper with the word 'Help' written on it which was burning hot in her pocket. When she ventured inside she saw the glow of the candle in a small lantern which hung from one of the central roof beams. The roof was low, heavily beamed. The floor was swept clean and there were benches made from tree stumps, and rugs for sitting on forming a circle. In the middle of the circle was a flat stone.

Mason knelt on the wooden floor and frowned. 'Look at this,' he whispered, 'the floor is painted with patterns and markings in a sort of spiral.'

Summer was close to Mason and she crouched beside him, gazing at the strange markings. 'This place gives me the shivers,' she said. 'I think I'm going back outside.'

Charlie had sat himself down on one of the rugs and was examining a carved piece of wood he'd found on a stone shelf. He ran his fingers along the polished surface. The grain of

the wood was streaked blood red. 'Dad, what kind of wood is this?'

His father looked closely at the carving, ran his hand across it and nodded. 'Yew, I think it's a piece of yew. Beautifully carved isn't it?' He handed it back to Charlie.

Outside, Summer felt like a weight had lifted off her head and shoulders. She breathed the cool air and heard again the rush of water from the stream. She went round the side of the barn and found a path which led up through the trees. There were small wooden bridges across the stream and ahead she saw Harry standing on a stone bench. He was peering intently through the binoculars.

'Hey Harry,' she called, relieved that she wasn't alone.

'Hush a minute,' he said. 'I thought I saw someone moving on the path down there where we came from.'

'Who did you see?' asked Summer.

'I'm not sure. Looked like a girl, wearing a baseball cap.'

Summer stifled a gasp. 'Let me see.'

Harry shook his head. 'Whoever it was she's gone now.'

'Are you sure it was a girl?'

'Well it was a small person with a cap and a pony tail.'

Summer held back for a moment before she asked the next question. 'Was there a blue and yellow ribbon in her hair?'

'How did you know?' replied Harry staring at Summer.

She hesitated, then decided to tell him her secret about the girl at the hotel and the piece of paper.

Harry shrugged. 'I just don't know. Maybe she's a local girl who just wants to make friends.'

'But what about the paper and the word 'Help'?'

'Some sort of game, maybe, just to get your attention.'

Summer folded the paper and put it back in her pocket. She wasn't so sure it was that simple.

The adults had given them half an hour to explore the wood, then they were to meet back by the gate at the carved stone. Mason and

Charlie spent some time on the rope swing behind the barn. Max headed up the path which Harry and Summer had taken. But there was no sign of them. He crossed several small bridges, noted various posts marking the paths painted with different coloured dots and decided to follow the red ones.

It was not a dense wood. The trees were still quite young but even so you quickly felt the wood close around you. Max was glad of the painted markers even though, now and then, he could hear the distant sound of running feet and the faint shouts of Mason and Charlie on the rope swing.

He followed the path which meandered up the hillside through the trees and then, a short way ahead, he saw some sort of wooden structure. It was built on a wooden platform, like a miniature house with a steeply sloping roof and at the back a single door no higher than his shoulder. He opened the door. It was a little place for sitting with a single chair. Then he remembered. This must be another of those quiet places Victoria had told them to look out for.

He was just backing out through the door when his eye caught a slight movement under the wooden platform that the little house was built on. It was a piece of ribbon, blue and yellow striped, being blown by the breeze. He bent down and looked more closely. The ribbon was attached to a small backpack and there was a sleeping bag and a blanket. Maybe people camped here overnight sometimes and had left their gear for next time. It was one thing to come here during the day but Max didn't fancy the idea of being here alone at night.

He looked up at the sound of voices and footsteps running along a lower path. It was Charlie and Mason. He chased after them and was glad when the path emerged from the edge of the wood and he was back on the main path.

'What a place!' exclaimed Mason when he saw Max. 'We found this amazing tunnel of willow, a bit like a maze.'

'Mason thought we were lost,' said Charlie.

'No I didn't,' retorted Mason.

'I found this little shelter,' said Max, 'like a small house, just big enough for one person to sit in.'

'Was it made of gingerbread?' laughed Mason.

'No, really it was like a small house.'

'With tiny people living in it?'

'Oh shut up! I know what I saw,' replied Max, annoyed that his older brother wouldn't take him seriously.

Ahead of them, by the gate, they saw the parents waiting with Harry and Summer. They ran to join them.

'Okay, team, let's go,' said Charlie's mother and they set off back along the valley the way they had come.

From the upper branches of a gnarled oak tree, two eyes followed them until they disappeared among the trees which bordered the river. The eyes watched while small fingers twisted a piece of ribbon round a lock of blonde hair.

CHAPTER 4

The following morning the boys wanted to be on the water. On the map Charlie had spotted a small island a short distance from the beach at Glencoyne Bay which was just a brief car ride from the cottages. Between them, they had two paddleboards and a canoe. They'd done a number of small expeditions on the boards before, so the island was not going to be too far for them.

They loaded the cars, piled in and were soon down at the edge of Ullswater Lake. The adults set up camp and started inflating the boards and canoe while Summer and the boys explored the shoreline. There was little wind, the surface of Ullswater glinting silver in the early morning sunshine. At one end of the beach a stream fanned out over the stones and bubbled into the lake. In the other direction the beach narrowed.

Another family with three children and a small dog were already camped further down the beach. When Summer saw the dog she was immediately drawn towards it. She had a magnetic attraction for dogs but was constantly being warned by her parents to be careful to ask permission of the owners before she put out a hand to stroke their dog. It was a Labrador puppy, playful and eager for stroking. While Summer knelt near the dog she watched the children, an older boy and two small girls, moving away from the shore. The boy was kneeling at the back of the paddleboard and using a long paddle while the two girls were lying nearer the front, paddling the water with their hands.

Further out she could see Charlie and Max on one paddleboard heading for the island with Mason and Harry following on the second. Harry's father was in the canoe at a distance as

backup. Summer wished she was with them but she'd been slow to make a decision. She ran back along the beach and found Mason's binoculars. At least she could follow their progress and feel she was part of the fun. She looked beyond them at the island. From what she could see it was just a rounded hump of rock with a small tree and some bushes on one side.

Charlie had a better view now that he and Max were getting closer.

'What d'you think?' asked Max. 'Looks quite steep on this side.'

Charlie nodded.

The island was sheer on two sides and would be difficult to make a landing but as they paddled round the far side Max saw that the rock sloped down to a ledge just above the water level. 'Hey, this is better,' he shouted.

'Yes, we'll pull in here,' agreed Charlie.

They beached the paddleboard and looked back over the water towards the shore.

They'd paddled a fair distance. Mason and Harry arrived and hopped off their board.

'Hey, that was pretty easy,' remarked Harry. He looked around the small hump of rock which was their island. 'D'you reckon we could camp out here sometime? There's space for a small tent near that tree.'

'And you'd get some shelter from those bushes,' added Max.

The tree was a gnarled hawthorn, windswept, shorn of its lower branches and forming a tight cluster of twisted greenery. There was a flat area of rock, wide enough to take a small tent, then some thorn bushes and a sheer rock face which rose to the domed peak of the island. Max was already starting to climb the slope up to the peak.

'Great view from here,' he called when he finally reached the highest point.

Harry's father in the canoe had gone round the far side of the island.

Summer could see Max waving from the highest point. She refocused the binoculars and scanned slowly down to watch Mason and Charlie on another part of the island.

It was then she heard the scream. She looked up to see the boy on the other paddle board waving his arms. She fixed the binoculars on them and could see the boy lying on the paddleboard reaching out towards the girls who had fallen into the water. She realised their screams were not in fun but in panic!

'Dad, quick, I think they're in trouble!'

Summer's father looked to where the two girls were thrashing the water with their arms. They weren't too far from the island. He whistled and waved his arms to attract the attention of Charlie and the others. Max heard the whistle and then heard the screams from the paddle board which was a short distance away. 'Hey boys,' he said, 'I think they need our help!'

Charlie and Max were quick to launch their board and Mason and Harry followed. The canoe was out of sight round the other side of the island.

Charlie knelt on the front of the board and dug deep with his paddle to get it going. Max did the same behind him. Then they used quick light strokes to power the board forward. Charlie could see the boy on the board some way ahead. The boy couldn't reach the girls who were sinking under the water. At times only their arms were visible then for a moment their heads would appear. They didn't seem to be wearing life-jackets.

Mason was paddling as fast as he could while Harry lay on the front ready to try to grab the girls. From his standing position Mason could clearly see there wasn't much time left before the girls went under completely.

The boys quickly closed in on the girls and Charlie and Mason dived off their boards to grab hold of the girls' arms. Max steadied himself and leaned out to grab the collar of Charlie's life jacket while Harry reached out to grab Mason. Charlie grasped the arm of one of the girls and Mason took hold of the other girl. Their brother was sobbing and thumping the surface of his board. It had all happened so quickly and he hadn't known what to do.

The two girls were choking up water as Charlie and Mason dragged them with Max's help onto the paddleboards.

Both boys were gasping for breath. Harry helped to heave them out of the water.

'Well done, guys,' said Max. 'They're going to be okay.'

The girls' panic subsided and they just lay there whimpering. Their brother was still sobbing with relief. 'I've lost my paddle,' he wailed.

'We'll have to tow their board with the canoe,' said Max. He waved as Harry's dad paddled towards them. 'We're okay,' he called. 'Let's put the girls in the canoe for safety.'

'Panic over,' nodded Charlie, patting Mason on the back. 'Well done, coz.'

'Team effort,' said Mason.

Harry attached a line from the canoe to the front of the boy's paddleboard and they started towing it towards the shore where his parents were standing hugging each other.

Summer had watched it all. She had gripped tighter and tighter on the binoculars as she watched the drama unfolding before her eyes. It was like watching a dramatic movie, but this was real and her brothers' and cousins' lives were being tested.

She raised her fist in the air when she saw Max and Charlie waving as they paddled slowly towards the shore. 'Yay, boys,' she shouted, 'you did it! That was an amazing rescue.' She ran down to the water and hugged each one of them.

The parents of the girls helped their three children ashore and laid them down on towels and covered them in blankets. Their little dog snuffled close to them.

The father shook his head. 'Boys, we can't thank you enough.'

'They should have had life-jackets,' said Charlie.

'I know,' replied the man. 'That was stupid of me.'

'We only just got there in time.'

'What can we do to thank you?' asked the mother.

'Just get them life-jackets!' said Mason, annoyed that some parents could be so foolish.

The boys pulled the boards along the shoreline, back to their camp at the other end of the beach. Their parents had towels ready and there were hugs all round. Harry's mother clapped her hands. 'That was brilliant. Well done, boys.'

'Such quick thinking,' added Mason's father. 'I think you saved some lives today.'

'It's all about good timing,' said Harry shrugging. 'Right people, right place.'

His father smiled, nodded and gave Harry a huge hug.

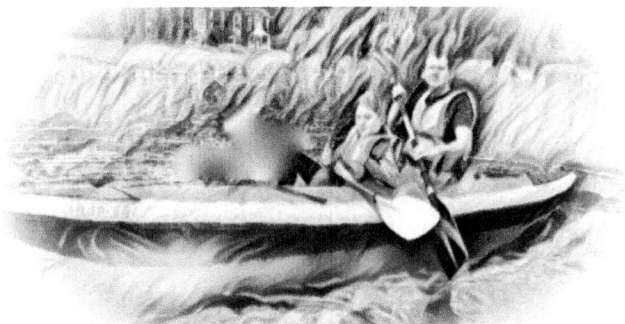

CHAPTER 5

The den was taking shape. It was the obvious place. The fallen tree on the hillside overlooking the cottages formed a perfect arch and it was easy to see how they could weave a roof from bracken and lean branches against the main trunk to form the sloping sides of the den. Mason had been studying it ever since they arrived and worked out how to engineer the job.

He'd asked Max to collect bracken which Max found quite easy; the stiff stalks pulled out of the ground cleanly and the fronds could be woven to create a dense covering. Charlie was finding lengths of fallen branches and Summer was clearing the inside to create space for sleeping bags. They were intent on sleeping out in the den for at least one night.

Harry was leaning against the wall which bordered the field. He was supposed to be collecting tree branches but he would rather be scanning the fences and sky with the binoculars, hoping to see something unusual. As yet, he'd spotted no red kites or eagles, but there was always a solitary buzzard, sometimes two, gliding in circles above Gowbarrow Fell.

The sound of a rock being dislodged stopped him for a moment. It came from behind the wall. He waited, listened, keeping very still. There was the sound of footsteps moving away.

He jumped up and stood on a rock to see who it was. It was the girl with the baseball cap again. 'Hey,' he called. 'Hey, wait a minute.'

She turned, hesitated and stood still, fingers twirling the ribbon in her hair. She wore denim dungarees and a yellow tee shirt. Harry started to move towards her.

'I just wanted to speak to you.'

The girl looked away. 'So what d'you want with me?' she said defiantly.

Harry walked to the gate in the wall and climbed over. Now he could see her more clearly. She looked about his age. She was skinny and long legged. Cap, blonde hair in a pony tail tied back with a blue and yellow striped ribbon.

Now Harry remembered. 'I've seen you before. You were at Lucy's Wood two days ago.'

'What if I was. It's a free country!'

'And you were at the hotel when we were eating there. You gave a note to my cousin.'

At that point the girl's defiance melted a little and she dropped her head and looked away.

'My cousin was worried by your note. What did it mean - 'Help'?'

The girl looked down at the ground and shook her head. 'Just a silly game,' she murmured and she started picking at the moss on the wall. 'Sometimes you need a friend. Your cousin looked like a fun person.'

'She is,' said Harry. 'Her name's Summer. My name's Harry. What's your name?'

'Sophya,' replied the girl.

'You're not English.' Harry had noted the unusual lilt in her voice.

'I'm from Ukraine.'

'Of course, the blue and yellow stripes in your ribbon. I knew I'd seen it before on the flags.'

'I escaped from the war,' said the girl, 'with my mother. She works at the hotel.'

Harry nodded. He wondered about her father but the girl read his thoughts.

'My father's in the army. He was an engineer but then he volunteered.'

'D'you hear from him?'

'Not often. My mother's worried he's been taken prisoner, but we don't know for sure.'

It seemed childish now to mention the den but Harry was stumped as to what to say to the girl. 'We're building a den, down in the field. D'you want to come and see it. Meet the others?'

Sophya hesitated and then gave a nod.

Harry went on. 'Sounds a bit silly, building a den when your father's fighting in a real war.'

'In the army they're always building dens to hide from the Russians. Building a den's not silly.'

They walked down the field to the fallen tree. The others stopped what they were doing and stared at the girl. Summer hadn't seen them at first as she'd been inside the den. When she came out she said, 'Oh! It's my friend with the ribbon. Hallo, I'm Summer. Where did Harry find you?'

The girl blushed a little at the word 'friend'. Harry sensed her awkwardness. 'We just met up on the path. This is Sophya. She's from Ukraine.'

'Where the war is?' exclaimed Max.

'Sophya and her mother escaped from the war. Her father's in the army still fighting over there,' Harry explained.

'Wow,' said Max, 'that's amazing.'

Sophya was keen to change the subject. 'I like your den. It looks well built.'

'Come and look inside,' said Summer. 'I've been making it tidy.'

They all crawled inside. It was something of a squash but that helped to ease the tension as they nudged against each other to find a space.

'You speak good English,' commented Mason. 'Where did you learn?'

'In school and in Ukraine we see movies in English, we hear music with English words. I like Ed Sheeran and Dua Lipa.'

'I can play some Ed Sheeran on the piano,' said Harry.

'You play piano? So do I. Or I used to. My street got bombed and my poor piano got smashed up for fire wood. It was so sad.'

'Maybe after the war you'll get a new piano,' said Summer.

Sophya nodded. 'Maybe.'

'So how did you come to be in the Lake District?' asked Charlie. 'It's not an obvious place to come to.'

'We were first in London. But we hated it. Too many people. Too much noise. Then my mother saw an advert for the job at the hotel. We got on a train with our two bags a few weeks ago and arrived here.'

'Different from London,' said Charlie.

'Very different. A bit lonely but much better.'

'We're going sailing this afternoon,' said Harry.

'Yes, dad's hired a sailboat for the afternoon,' added Mason. 'Will you come with us?'

'I'll have to tell my mother where I'm going. She worries I'm going to get kidnapped.'

'What, here?' Charlie frowned.

'My mother worries about everything.'

CHAPTER 6

The sailing centre was at the south end of
the lake in the village of Glenridding. It was close
to the pier where the lake steamers docked. The
car was parked and they made their way down
to where the boats were moored.

Harry was walking alongside Sophya. 'So
when I saw you at Lucy's Wood, were you
following us?'

Sophya pushed her hands further into the
pockets of her dungarees and kicked at a stone.
She shrugged. 'Not exactly. I had heard your
voices. I was curious.'

Harry nodded. 'Go on.'

'They were happy voices. I have not
heard happy voices for a long time. In Ukraine
there were no happy voices and on the train

across Europe everyone was so sad to be leaving their homes and so frightened. And then in London my mother was always worried and always ready to cry.'

'What about your friends at home? What about school?'

'My school was bombed. I haven't seen or heard from my friends for many months.'

Harry felt out of his depth. He'd never met anyone who was suffering with so many worries. 'Have you ever been sailing before?'

Sophya nodded. 'Where I lived, in Odesa, it was by the sea and my father had a sailboat. We would sail out from the harbour there in the summer. I learnt how to steer the boat, to watch the wind, to raise and lower the sails.'

They reached the dockside and were taken along the jetty to where the boat was tied up. It was a wooden, clinker built boat with rust-red sails. 'It's like in *Swallows and Amazons*,' remarked Charlie.

'What is that?' asked Sophya.

'Oh, it's a children's book. It's about some children who get caught up in an adventure,' explained Charlie. 'One group has a boat called *Swallow* and the others have a boat called *Amazon*. And their boats are just like this one.'

'I'm going to be captain and sit at the front,' said Summer.

'Can I sit with you?' asked Sophya.

Summer nodded and smiled. 'We have to hold on tight.'

They were given life jackets and when they were all properly equipped they climbed down into the boat. Mason's father checked that they were positioned so that the boat was balanced before untying the rope from the dock and getting in to take the helm.

Summer sat close to Sophya. 'Are you scared? I've never been in a sailboat like this before.'

Sophya shook her head. 'Don't worry, hold on to me and you'll be safe.' She was used to trying to keep people safe - little children, babies, old people who'd been blasted out of their homes - she had looked after them all in different situations. It was such a relief to be free of those worries.

There was a light breeze blowing down the lake so first they had to tack towards the western shore and then back across to the opposite shore to make headway up the lake. The red sails curved and the old boat heeled a little causing them all to shift and for Summer to squeal with a mixture of excitement and slight fear. She gripped Sophya's arm. 'I'm glad you came with us.'

'I'm glad too,' nodded Sophya and she closed her eyes and felt the warm breeze on her face and the sun on her eyelids. For a moment she was back in Odesa with her father before the war - the gentle lift of the wind along the edge of the sail, the ripple of water beneath the hull.

They sailed past a small rocky island and then Max pointed. 'There's our island, see it with the trees and the rocky top where I stood.'

'It's called Norfolk Island on this map,' said Mason, poring over an OS map he'd brought, 'and this little rocky one we just passed..'

'Covered in bird poo,' added Charlie.

'It's called….'

'Bird poo island.'

'Well maybe it should be, but its real name is Wall Holm, and across there, that rocky headland is Devil's Chimney.'

'You see, Sophya, Mason's our local travel guide. It can get a bit boring at times,' said Charlie.

'Just helping your education,' replied Mason.

Mason's father steered the boat close up to Norfolk Island.

'We didn't really get a chance to explore the island last time, did we,' commented Harry.

'I like this island. If I need to escape and hide out somewhere this would be a good place.' Sophya murmured this more to herself than to anyone else.

'Why would you need to escape and hide?' whispered Summer.

'I always need to think about these things,' replied Sophya, which left Summer rather puzzled and Harry frowning.

They spent some time on the island before setting off to the other side of the lake. One of the Ullswater steamers was ploughing a white furrow down the centre of the lake.

'Look out for the waves from the wake,' shouted Mason's father and sure enough, within a few minutes, a series of waves passed under the sailboat causing it to dip and lift. There were squeals from Summer as she clung on to Sophya's arm.

'Wow, that was scary,' she said.

Sophya smiled and patted Summer's hand.

Mason was studying the map again. 'If you steer round that headland, which is called Silver Point, there should be a beach at Silver Bay. We could have our picnic there.'

His father nodded and tightened the sail to head up closer into the wind. The sailboat heeled again and the bubbling wake spread out behind them. The clear sky of the morning was changing to thickening cloud which was misting the tops of some of the higher mountains. There was more of a breeze now and the sailboat responded quickly with a surge of speed.

Rounding the headland they could see the bay and a beach of fine shingle. The boat nosed towards the beach and they tied up to the trunk of a small tree which overhung the water. Then they had to jump from the boat into the water which was knee deep. They headed for a grassy mound where they set up camp.

'Right, I'll get the scran,' said Charlie, and he started unpacking the sandwiches and drinks from the backpacks.

'What is 'scran'?' asked Sophya.

'It's what they call food or a snack in the north of England,' replied Charlie.

'A new word for me,' she nodded.

It was at that moment that a sound like distant thunder started to rumble from the north end of the lake. The sound deepened like a far off echo in the cavern of the sky.

'Jets!' shouted Max.

The booming crescendo of noise was as if the sky was being hollowed out. They saw the

speck coming towards them, the sound changing to an ear-splitting hissing like water gushing.

'F-16!' Max shouted, pointing.

The grey fighter jet flashed past and disappeared round the curve in the valley, dragging with it a slipstream of thunderous noise.

'There's another coming,' cried Max. 'They often come in twos. Listen!'

All eyes were looking down the lake. All eyes were glued to the sky. All eyes except those of Sophya. No-one had noticed or heard her scream, had seen her crouch on the ground, her hands over her ears, her head shaking from side to side. She curled into a ball, her hands clasped over her head, her body jerking in quick spasms.

The second jet screamed past them, thunder drumming at their ears, the air of the valley sucked away, and then the roar fading.

'That second one was a Typhoon,' cried Max. 'Different wing shape, like a triangle. Wow, that was fantastic!'

It was Summer who noticed first. 'Dad, what's happened to Sophya?'

The others looked at the curled body of the girl, quivering and jerking. She was sobbing and murmuring words they didn't understand. Summer's father bent over her, his hand resting lightly on her head. 'Just give her some time to recover,' he said. 'She's been in a war, remember. The sound of jet planes probably brings back some terrible memories. She'll be okay.'

After a few minutes, Sophya's breathing quietened and the shivering stopped. She went into a light sleep.

Summer sat close beside her, eyes moist with tears.

'We have no idea what she's been through,' said Harry.

'And her father's still in the middle of it,' added Charlie. 'We're so lucky, aren't we.'

Max was very quiet. He'd found it so exciting to really see these planes that he had models of at home and that he'd read about. He'd found pictures of them, cut them out and stuck them in his war scrap book. He knew the facts about speeds, firepower, how superb they were in dogfights. He'd watched the movie *Top Gun Maverick* with pilots doing amazing things in similar fighter jets. But now, seeing Sophya curled in a ball, sobbing on the ground, it didn't feel quite so exciting anymore.

Sailing back to the dock at Glenridding was more comfortable than earlier as there was a following wind. The main sail was out wide, the wind pushing the boat forward in a smooth glide through the water. Sophya leaned her arm against the boom of the sail and rested her head against it. Summer sat next to her and kept looking and checking Sophya's face. All she saw was the eyes staring ahead looking at nothing in particular. She had not spoken since coming round from the trauma of hearing the jets fly past.

'Why do they fly here in such a beautiful place and fly so low?' she murmured to Charlie who sat near her.

He was relieved to hear her voice again. 'They use it for training. It happens quite often, I think.'

Sophya shook her head. 'I think it's horrible.'

'I suppose they have to be ready for what they have to go and face,' replied Charlie, 'anywhere in the world.'

There was a slight nod of agreement from Sophya. 'Such a shock, that's all.'

After they had docked, they drove back to the cottages and then Mason's father took Sophya back to the hotel to let her mother know what had happened. Summer insisted she went too and she held Sophya's hand as they went up the drive to the front door of the hotel.

Hearing about the events, Sophya's mother went to put her arms round her daughter but Sophya pulled back. 'I'm okay mama, it was just a shock. Don't get upset. I'm okay.'

'Thank you for keeping her safe,' said her mother. She looked down at Summer. 'And I'm glad she found a new friend.'

Summer smiled. 'We'll look after her.'

The mother nodded. 'I'm sure you will. Thank you.'

# CHAPTER 7

The following morning was grey with a light drizzle in the air, not a day to be outside. Mason was cross-legged in a corner of the sofa, head in his latest Harry Potter book, Max was lying on the floor sketching. Summer was colouring a picture and Harry was working on a magic trick with some playing cards

Charlie was giggling to himself as he worked through a joke book. 'Okay, listen up. What did one wall say to the other wall?' He waited for some response. There was none. 'I'll meet you at the corner!' he grinned looking round. No-one had looked up. 'Okay, how about this one: What has four wheels and flies?'

'A garbage truck,' groaned Harry. 'Heard it before. Can't you find something original?'

Charlie flicked through the joke book. 'Okay how about this - What d'you call cheese that isn't yours?'

'Don't know,' muttered Harry.

'Nacho cheese!' giggled Charlie.

'Slightly better,' nodded Harry.

There was a knock on the outer door. Harry opened it to see Sophya, hair damp from the rain. She was wearing a blue denim jacket and shouldering a small backpack.

'Hey, it's Sophya,' he called out to the others. 'Come in. How are you?'

She nodded. 'Better. Thank you.' The others looked up as she came into the room.

'I came to thank you all for looking after me yesterday. I brought you something.' She unzipped her back pack and took out a long tin. 'Mama and I made this for you. It's a special cake like we have back in Ukraine.'

Mason's father looked in. 'Hi, Sophya.'

'She brought us a cake from Ukraine,' said Harry, 'well not exactly from Ukraine but like they have in Ukraine.'

'It's called 'makivnik' but I think you would call it Poppy cake. If you cut it you'll see,' explained Sophya.

Harry fetched a knife from the kitchen and Max brought plates. He cut a few slices. The centre of the cake was a spiral of poppy seeds mixed with honey and raisins.

Max leaned forward. He could smell the sweetness. 'Wow, looks yummy.'

'My mother bakes good cakes,' Sophya nodded, 'and I'm learning too. She makes them for the tea in the afternoon at the hotel. People seem to like them.'

'I'm not surprised,' said Mason. 'This tastes really good.'

'What are you all doing?' asked Sophya, taking off her jacket and squatting down on the carpet.

'Charlie's telling boring jokes,' moaned Harry.

'Better than wasting time on magic tricks that don't work,' replied Charlie. 'How boring is that!'

Sophya smiled. 'Please tell me one of your jokes, Charlie.'

'Okay,' said Charlie, 'how about this. How do you tell the difference between a bull and a cow?'

Sophya shrugged. 'I don't know.'

'It's either one or the udder,' grinned Charlie.

Sophya frowned and shook her head. 'I don't understand.'

Mason's father put his head round the door. 'Don't forget, English is Sophya's second language and these are puns which makes it tricky.'

'Okay, try this one. What's red and smells like blue paint?'

Sophya shrugged again.

'Red paint!' grinned Charlie triumphantly.

Sophya nodded and smiled. 'I think I get that one.'

'No more jokes, please Charlie,' said Harry.

Sophya glanced down at Max's sketch book. 'Can I look at your drawings?'

Max closed the book. 'I'm not sure you'd be interested.'

'I like drawing too,' she said as she took up the book and started turning the pages.

Page after page showed battles with soldiers shooting at each other, planes with swastikas on the wings dropping bombs, ships sinking with smoke spiralling up into the sky.

'It's all about war,' frowned Sophya. 'Why do you draw pictures of war?'

Max just shook his head but said nothing.

'And are these German planes dropping bombs and are these English soldiers?'

Max nodded.

'But the Germans are our friends. They are not fighting anyone. These should be Russian planes. They're the ones dropping bombs.'

'It's the second world war,' said Max.

'But that was so long ago in history. Why do you still want to even think about it. Wars are horrible, horrible!'

'I'm sorry,' mumbled Max.

'Why not draw about peaceful things; birds, flowers, animals, that kind of thing?' She looked at Max whose head had dropped. 'I have a sketch book of war,' she said. 'I will show it to you one day. When I was down in the shelter and we could hear the bombs falling on Odesa, blowing up our houses, I drew pictures of people's faces, their tears, pictures of buildings after the bombs had fallen, pictures of cars burning. That was real war, not make-believe war.'

Summer was looking at Max, she saw the frown on his face. 'We don't know much about your war,' she said to Sophya.

Sophya nodded slowly. 'No, of course, how could you know about it?'

'I'd like to see your drawings,' said Harry. 'I like drawing birds and animals, but especially birds. Eagles and owls are my favourite.'

'Sometimes, at night, I listen at my bedroom window to the night sounds. There are owls in the trees near the hotel.'

'What's it like living in a hotel?' asked Summer.

Sophya nodded. 'I like it. Mr Williams, the owner, is a kind man and the other people who work there are friendly. Someone new came last week, another chef. I think they said he was from Poland but I haven't really talked to him.'

Mason got up from the sofa. 'Hey, the rain's stopped. Shall we go and check how wet the den is? If we're going to sleep there it'll need to be dry.'

'Will you sleep in our den?' asked Summer, taking Sophya's hand as they went outside.

'I don't think so, I like my soft bed and my soft pillows too much. And I have bad dreams so I might keep you all awake.'

'What d'you dream about?'

Sophya shook her head. 'You don't need to know, just lots of things that make me wake up. It's better for me to sleep in my own bed.'

Summer nodded. 'I'd like to see it sometime. But now I have to go. Daddy's taking me to get my glasses fixed. One of the arms broke. So I'll see you another time. Bye.'

The others went out into the cottage yard. Mason and Max ran off up the hill to check on the den.

'Could I see your drawings sometime?' asked Harry.

Sophya nodded. 'Come now if you want to. My mother's busy in the kitchen preparing food for the day. And I know Mr Williams, the manager, won't mind.'

'I'll tag along too, if that's okay,' said Charlie.

*

At the back of the Royal Hotel was a small garden. A metal fire escape spiralled down from the upper floors. Sophya led the way up the steps to a side door. Inside, they went down a corridor and up some more steps where she stopped at one of the doors. She took a key from her pocket and unlocked the door and the boys followed her inside.

There was a small single bed, a chest of drawers, a dressing table with a mirror and some of Sophya's clothes draped over a chair. 'Welcome to my little home,' she said. There was a window seat with a flowery cushion. 'This is where I like to sit. I can hear the river, see the bridge and listen to the wind in the trees.'

'That's a nice view,' agreed Charlie. 'Have you tried to draw it?'

'Not yet. I have taken photographs with my little camera so I can look at them later and draw from them.' She went to the chest of drawers and from the top drawer took out her sketch book. It had a red cover, scuffed at the edges and blotched with ink stains and doodles. 'This is my sketch book. This is where I store some memories of Ukraine, not always good memories I have to say.' She knelt by the bed and laid down the book. Harry and Charlie crouched down on either side of her.

The first picture was of some boats moored at a quayside. 'This is at the port of Odesa where my home is. This was a week before the invasion.'

She turned a page. 'And this is my house. I don't know how damaged it is now, but this is how I remember it.' It was a simple sketch of a two storey house, white walls, an orange tiled roof and flower pots either side of the front door.

She turned another page. The next sketch showed a tank with a white Z on the back. A soldier with a gun leaned from the turret of the tank.

'My grandmother lives in the city of Kherson. We were visiting when the Russians came into the city. There were lines of tanks and other army trucks full of soldiers. People were standing in front of the tanks with flags. I took a photograph from my grandmother's window. She told me to stop and said that I could get arrested if the soldiers found out. But I didn't stop until she started crying, then I felt bad. I drew this later from the photograph. I have many photographs. I hid the little card from the camera in my shoe.' Sophya went to the chest of drawers and took out a canvas shoe. She showed the boys the little space in the heel of the shoe and took out the camera card.

'Did you use charcoal for this drawing?' asked Harry.

Sophya nodded. 'There was lots of burnt wood lying around after the explosions and the fires. I used to collect small pieces which I would use for drawing, like with this one of the tank.'

'So what happened to the people in front of the tanks with their flags?' asked Charlie.

'When the Russians arrived, the people in the city came out in big crowds. They carried flags and chanted and stood in front of the tanks to stop them.'

'What happened then?'

'For a time it seemed the Russians did not know what to do. But then they started shooting, and the people ran for cover. That is when I left with my mother at night to get back to Odesa. It was not easy escaping the soldiers at the check points.'

She turned another page. 'This is in the shelter in Odesa when the bombs and missiles were falling on us.' The sketch showed the grim faces of people huddled together - mothers and babies, old people in blankets. Another sketch showed a bombed building with no roof and curtains hanging out of windows with broken glass.

'And this is the train we took when we left Odesa.'

'You and your mother are very brave,' said Charlie, 'to travel such a long way and leave your home and your grandmother.'

'D'you get news from her. Is she still alive?' asked Harry.

'She has been very sick but Kherson has now been liberated and she is much better. The Russians have gone but they did terrible things before they left, shooting and hurting people, stealing things, wrecking houses just for fun. I hate all Russians! I would kill if I met one!' she hissed through gritted teeth and with clenched fists.

Harry and Charlie were shocked by the force of Sophya's words and by the depth of her anger. And they were shocked by the images in the sketch book. This young girl, with her skinny legs and arms, with her blonde hair scraped back and tied with the striped blue and yellow ribbon, was like no-one they had ever met before.

Charlie shook his head. 'I don't know what to say. I've never seen anything like this.'

'You're very good at drawing,' said Harry. 'These pictures are amazing.'

'Thank you,' said Sophya. 'And thank you for wanting to come and see them.' She closed the sketch book. 'Maybe that is enough for one afternoon.'

They followed her out of the room and back down the fire escape. Charlie suddenly stopped, held up his hand for a moment. 'Listen, d'you hear a piano? Where's that coming from?'

Someone was playing a piece of classical music. It was coming from the building which extended from the rear of the hotel.

'That's the old ballroom,' said Sophya. 'It is not used anymore. I looked inside the other day. It is full of old chairs and tables and lots of spiders' webs.'

They peered through the dusty windows. In the far corner of the room, someone was seated at an old grand piano, head bent over the keyboard, hands moving smoothly over the keys. Sophya motioned to the boys to follow her. 'There's a door round the side,' she whispered.

She turned the door handle as quietly as she could but as she pulled, the old door creaked a little on rusty hinges. The three of them peered into the old ballroom. Shafts of sunlight showed up the dust haze in the air. They stepped gingerly into the room. The melody coming from the piano was gentle and soothing and continued until Harry tasted dust and coughed. The pianist turned, put his hands to his face, got up quickly and disappeared out of another side door.

'Who was that?' asked Harry.

Sophya shook her head. 'I'm not sure.'

Charlie was frowning. 'I wonder why he ran off.'

'I will ask my mother to find out which of the staff plays the piano.'

'A bit strange, though, to disappear like that,' added Harry.

'But he could certainly make beautiful music,' said Sophya.

# CHAPTER 8

The holiday fell half way between Mason's and the twins' birthdays and Max's and Summer's birthdays later in the year. Now that they were all together they asked if they could have a general birthday celebration. On the menu at the hotel Summer had read about the 'High Tea'. She liked the sound of it, sitting on high bar stools, eating snacks and looking down on everyone else.

'No, it's not about sitting up high,' said her mother, 'it's about it being a special tea with special things to eat.'

'High class,' said Max laughing, 'not sitting on a high chair.'

'Well I didn't know,' said Summer. 'Anyway, shall we do it? Shall we have a High Tea for our birthdays, boys?'

'Sounds good,' nodded Harry.

'I'll phone and book it then,' said her mother.

The following afternoon they all walked down to the hotel. It was warm and sunny and a long table had been set up outside on the lawn. Sophya was there to meet them. 'Mama says the new Polish chef, his name is Mikolaj, but I call him Miki, does super Polish food. He's going to try some out on you for your birthday tea.'

'High Tea,' corrected Summer.

Sophya nodded. 'High Tea.'

'Did you ask your mother about the mystery piano player?' asked Charlie.

'I did, but so far she has not found out who it is.'

'What about the new chef, Miki?' suggested Harry.

Sophya shrugged. 'The problem there, is that Miki has a speech problem, he does not speak much. Something to do with his throat.'

'But she could still ask him.'

'Mama says that although he is a brilliant chef, he is very shy and keeps to himself.'

'Oh well, we'll just have to ambush the mystery player next time we hear the mystery piano in the haunted ballroom,' said Charlie.

'Which haunted ballroom?' asked Summer.

'He's joking,' said Sophya. 'There is an old ballroom which is not used anymore at the back of the hotel. It is kind of dark and spooky and that is where we saw someone playing the piano. But we do not know who it was.'

'That is kind of spooky,' nodded Mason, 'a phantom piano player in a haunted ballroom. I like the sound of that.'

A young waitress and a waiter finished setting out plates and cutlery on a long table and then Sophya's mother, Anna, came out and greeted them.

'How nice to meet you all,' she said. 'Please sit down. Now I must tell you the food will be new to you. Our new chef, Mikolaj, has done special Polish food from his homeland.

There will be little signs giving the Polish name of the food on each dish. He hopes you will enjoy it.'

There were 'Happy Birthday' banners strung above the table and party hats for everyone. Drinks were served and then the first plates of food arrived.

Harry read from the little flag sign stuck to a plate of golden croquettes. '*Polish Hush Puppies,*' he said. 'I thought Hush Puppies were some kind of shoes.'

'I've got something called *Kielbasa Sliders*,' said Mason, reading from the little paper flag. These were tiny filled bread rolls held down with a cocktail stick. Another sign read *Klopsiki*, which were tiny meat balls. Next, there were *Pierogi,* little dumplings filled with jam, *Paszteciki,* tiny meat rolls and then plates of sweet *Chrusciki,* angel wing cakes. Finally *Racuchy Pancakes* made with apples and sprinkled with icing sugar.

'You have to try something from every plate,' insisted Max's mother, 'before you can have a slice of birthday cake.'

And so the High Tea began. There were frowns and hesitant tastings of food which looked unfamiliar but once tasted, they realised Polish food could be delicious.

After about an hour, Max patted his stomach. 'Wow, I'm stuffed,' he said. 'That was an amazing tea.'

Finally there was a cheer as two birthday cakes were brought in with candles flickering on the top. One was for the boys and one for Summer.

Her eyes glowed as she gazed at the candles.

'Blow them out and make a wish,' urged Max.

Summer hesitated for a moment and then blew them out in one go. The boys blew out theirs and everyone clapped.

'And now we should congratulate the chef,' said Max's mother and she called to the young waitress. 'Could you ask the chef to come out for a moment, please?'

But it was Sophya's mother who emerged from the hotel first. She nodded. 'Miki is a little shy but he will be out in a moment.' She looked round the faces at the table. 'So how did you like your Polish high tea?'

'It was so yummy,' replied Summer, 'I tried everything, which is not what I usually do.'

They turned to see a tall young man with dark brown hair and fair skin, wearing a white chef's overall and apron standing just outside the door of the hotel. He bowed several times as everyone clapped. He placed his hand over his heart and bowed again. Then he turned and went back inside. 'That is our new chef, Mikolaj,' said Sophya's mother. 'A young man of few words but a master baker and chef, I think you will agree?'

'Thank you for our tea,' said Max, 'it was different but I liked it.'

'Our pleasure,' nodded Anna. 'The manager, Mr Williams, will be very pleased.' She waved, turned and went back inside the hotel.

'So, who's for a game of chess?' asked Mason, looking across the garden to the giant chess board on the lawn.

'We're there,' said Charlie. 'Me, Sophya and Max are black, you, Summer  and Harry can be white.'

'You're on,' said Mason, 'and you're gonna get whupped!'

# CHAPTER 9

The clock at the side of Sophya's bed showed 5 a.m. Weak sunlight was filtering into the room where she lay exhausted. She had kicked the covers off and her arms had thrashed at the air where the swarms of drones had been attacking her. It was a recurring dream, to see those spider like machines whirring towards her, the noise like so many whining mosquitoes. The sound had seemed so real but she knew it was just the old nightmare returning. Drones had become a part of her life back home. The Ukrainian soldiers practised with them to seek out the enemy before flying them at the front line. When Russian drones came over it either meant a missile was about to explode or they were spying out the land before the shelling began. Whoever was flying them, when you saw them you knew it was a sign of serious danger.

Sophya stared at the ceiling, traced the cracks in the plaster trying to banish the image of the drones and the whine of their engines. She got out of bed, went over to the window seat and looked out. There was movement, a man crossing the bridge, heading up the path which led to the valley and Lucy's Wood. He had a backpack on and wore a jacket of that camouflage material that fishermen and hunters wear. He carried a fishing rod and on his head he wore a black beanie hat.

Half a mile away, Max stood at his bedroom window. He always woke early and although his parents encouraged him to sleep longer, he could never go back to sleep. He was immediately restless to be getting up, checking things out. But this morning he had been woken by a strange sound, the whirring of a small engine in the air above the cottages. He had looked out to see a small drone flying just above the trees towards the valley where the Aira river ran. He stood at the window wondering why anyone would be flying a drone so early in the morning. He got dressed quickly, went downstairs and out into the yard. He would just go to the top of the field and see if he could hear or see it.

Sophya stood at the top of the fire escape and looked beyond the trees towards the valley. She would take a walk to wake herself up and banish the fragments of her nightmares from her mind. She crossed the bridge and headed up the lane which followed the course of the river, wondering whether she would encounter the person with the beanie hat.

Towards the top of the hill where the path to Lucy's Wood branched down to the river and the trees, she stopped. She could hear running footsteps, the squeak of the hinges of a gate and then who should appear on the lane but Max.

'Max, why are you out so early?'

Max was startled to see Sophya. 'Why are you out as well?'

'Oh, I slept badly, and was having nightmares about hearing drones swarming round my bedroom.'

'But I was woken by the sound of a drone and then I just caught sight of it passing over the trees and flying up the valley.'

'So I didn't just dream it, I must have heard it too,' said Sophya.

Max held up his hand. 'Wait, listen, there it is again. It's coming back this way.'

They looked towards the trees at the start of the valley and saw the speck, like an angry insect, rising over the peak of the nearby hill, whirring away to the east and disappearing in the direction of Gowbarrow Fell.

'How weird,' said Max, 'to be flying a drone so early in the morning.'

'And why here,' said Sophya, 'over Lucy's Wood and then back again? Did you see a man in a black beanie hat and a green jacket?'

'I haven't seen anyone,' replied Max.

'He was going in the same direction as the drone, but he was carrying a fishing rod so was probably just doing early morning fishing.'

Max shook his head. 'It's all a bit weird.' Then he said, 'Have you been to Lucy's Wood and seen in the barn?'

'I know the wood but I haven't been in the barn. Maybe we could all go later when the others are up.'

Max nodded. 'Yes, I'd better get back in case someone finds my bed empty and wonders where I am.'

'See you later, then,' said Sophya and she waved and headed back down the lane.

At breakfast Max told the others about the drone and about meeting Sophya.

'She hasn't seen Lucy's Barn, so I said we'd meet her and take her there.'

'What kind of drone was it?' asked Mason.

'It was bigger than the small toy ones you can buy. Maybe like those ones hospitals use for sending medicines to other hospitals.'

'If we slept out in the den, maybe we could hear if the drone goes over again,' suggested Charlie.

'Good idea,' agreed Mason.

'But I'm having a sleepover with Sophya,' said Summer, 'so I won't be sleeping in the den. I'll be at the hotel.'

'There'll be other nights for sleeping out. Don't worry, you won't be missing anything,' said Harry. 'It's doubtful the drone will be flying over again. Probably was a one off.'

When breakfast was cleared, they left the cottages and headed up the field, past the den and found the path to the valley. They met Sophya on the lane and then went through the gate, down the meadow and into the trees which bordered the river.

'Did you see Beanie Man again?' asked Harry.

Sophya frowned. 'Beanie Man?' Then she nodded. 'Oh Max told you about the fisherman I saw.' She shook her head. 'No, I didn't see him.

Just a local man going fishing, I think. In Ukraine they go fishing early before the sun is too high. Must be a good time to go. Probably the same here.'

They emerged from the trees and crossed the meadow which led to the gate and the sign for Lucy's Wood.

'So where does the name come from - Lucy's Wood ?' asked Sophya.

Mason explained about the young girl who died and how her parents planted the wood and converted the barn. 'It's meant to be a place of happiness, but I think it's sad and Summer finds the barn a bit spooky,' said Mason.

'Back home, people plant trees for people who've died but I never heard of people planting a whole wood for someone.'

They arrived at the point where the side path branched up and into the trees. Once

through the trees they could see the barn up ahead. Close to the barn there were prayer flags in different colours, some on poles, others looped from tree to tree, all being moved by the breeze.

Max and Harry headed for the rope swing in the pine trees behind the barn. Charlie went to the barn and opened the heavy wooden door.

Inside, the candle was burning in the lantern and the sunlight was shafting through the slit windows in the walls lighting up the patterns on the wooden floor. It was very quiet.

Sophya sat on one of the wooden benches. Tears formed in her eyes and she covered her face with her hands. She sobbed quietly. After a few minutes she lifted her head and wiped her eyes with her sleeve. 'This is a sad place,' she murmured. 'Makes me think of home and all my friends and family who I may never see again.'

Summer came and sat beside her and rested her hand on Sophya's arm. Charlie stood behind her, feeling awkward about Sophya's sadness but not knowing quite how to comfort her. Very gently, he put his hand on her shoulder for a moment.

'I try not to think too much about what's happening at home, and where my papa is, but this place is so quiet.'

'D'you get any news about home?' asked Charlie.

Sophya nodded. 'We get little bits of news. My mother phones and sometimes gets through. We get text messages but people never really tell you the truth of how bad it is. But I just remember those Russian soldiers; they were like dark monsters with their black helmets, their face masks, the sound of their boots, their guns and knives - like something from a horror movie but it was all so real and horrible, and until this moment I had not been remembering it so clearly.'

'Maybe you should go out into the sunshine,' suggested Charlie, 'and try the swing. Take your mind off things.'

'Thanks, Charlie, good idea,' Sophya nodded and got up. She took Summer's hand in hers and gave her a quick hug. 'Thanks, my little friend, for being with me.'

'That's okay,' said Summer.

They all wandered down the hill from the barn, past the ponds and further down to the river itself in the bottom of the valley. There was a gate and next to the gate a pillar with a recess in which there was a copper cylinder with words on it. Behind it a small bell. Mason spun the cylinder to read the words on it. '*Peace I give unto you,* it says.'

Max found a stick and tapped the bell. It gave a dull ring.

'Looks like the kind of bell you see in a church,' said Sophya, 'or maybe in a Buddhist

temple.'

They all passed through the gate and Harry pointed. 'Look at this. It's a series of circles, no it's a spiral, edged with rocks. You start from the outside and as you go round you finally end up at that stone by the little fir tree in the middle.'

Summer made her way round the spiral and finally arrived at the middle. 'Yay!' she shouted standing by the keystone.

Sophya clapped. 'Now you have to make a wish, cos this is a place of magic.'

It was a strange place, an unusual place with its signs and symbols, its patterns carved into rocks, its prayer flags, some made ragged by the snatching of the wind.

There was a shout. It was Max, higher up the hill away from the river. 'Here, check this out!' he shouted, and he held something up in his hand.

'What is it?' asked Mason.

'It's a parachute, a tiny parachute,' called Max.

'Where did you find it?' asked Harry.

'Just in the grass over there. It's got numbers on it. Wonder what they mean?'

'Is it the kind of parachute drones use to drop things?' asked Mason.

'Was there anything attached to it?' said Harry.

'Nothing,' replied Max.

Mason was examining the parachute. 'It's well made. Designed to carry heavy objects maybe?'

'When you saw the drone this morning, was there anything hanging from it?' asked Charlie.

Max shook his head. 'Too far away to spot anything like that.'

'How odd,' commented Charlie.

'How spooky,' added Summer.

# CHAPTER 10

It was a dream about music, beautiful music, rising and falling, floating gently on the drifting waves of the dream. She opened her eyes. Summer was asleep beside her but it was still there, the music. Like the sound of the drone the previous morning, this was not in her dreams. This was real.

Sophya nudged Summer awake. 'Listen, it's the music again. The piano music like I heard with Harry and Charlie.'

'Where's it coming from?' asked Summer.

'The old ballroom. We need to go to the other door this time so that we can find out who it is before he escapes.'

They went quietly along the corridor, through the door which led to the fire escape and tiptoed down the steps. They made their way round the back of the hotel to the ballroom. The sound of the piano was more distinct now, it surged in waves of melody like the previous time. It was the same tune. Sophya remembered how it had made her feel emotional, kind of sad and happy at the same time.

They stood outside the door through which the pianist had escaped previously. Well, he won't escape this time, thought Sophya. They waited, listened to the piece of music building in a crescendo towards the end. When it finished, Sophya felt like clapping. So she did, but not before opening the door with a flourish. She stood clapping and looking open mouthed at the chef, Mikolaj. He put his hands to his mouth and gasped and shook his head.

'Miki, it was you! It was you I heard playing the other day. And you ran away before I could speak to you.'

He looked stunned and nervous.

'We love your playing,' said Summer. 'It is very beautiful.'

'Why did you run away?' asked Sophya.

He shrugged, pointed to his throat and shook his head.

Sophya nodded. 'Oh, I remember, you can't talk much.'

Mikolaj nodded.

'But there's nothing to be afraid of. You play so wonderfully.'

He put his hand across his heart and nodded, then put his hands together like in prayer and bowed his head a couple of times.

'What was the name of the piece you were playing?'

He mouthed some words, made a sound in his throat but then shook his head. He took a pen from his pocket, picked up a piece of old wallpaper which was lying on the lid of the piano and started writing.

Summer watched his hand with the pen slowly forming beautiful letters on the paper:

*RHAPSODY ON A THEME OF PAGANINI*
*by Sergei Rachmaninov*

Finally, he gave the piece of paper to Sophya.

She looked at the name *Rachmaninov.* 'What country was he from?'

Mikolaj dropped his head for a moment and coughed. Then he motioned for the paper. He wrote the word - *Russia.*

Sophya flinched. That such beauty could come from the country she loathed! 'I hate Russia!' she hissed. 'I hate Russians!'

Mikolaj's body swayed and he gripped the edge of the piano keyboard to steady himself.

Sophya felt bad at her outburst and touched him on his arm. 'But you play wonderfully and the music, even though, er it's Russian, is…' she shrugged, 'like nothing I've heard before. So thank you, and do not be afraid to play more. People would love to hear your playing.'

Again, his hand went across his heart and he nodded and gave a slight smile.

'Thank you,' said Summer, 'and thank you for that lovely food you made for my birthday.'

He nodded, put his hands together and bowed a couple of times.

Summer turned and went out through the door followed by Sophya.

'What a shame he can't speak. He seems a nice man,' said Summer.

Sophya agreed. 'He should not be so shy about playing the piano. Lots of people would like to hear his music, even if it is Russian.'

It was still very early and the two girls made their way back up to Sophya's room. The sound of someone having a shower in a room nearby meant they failed to hear another drone passing overhead.

But the boys had not missed it. They were quickly up and out of the den and running towards the valley following the sound. Mason levelled his binoculars and managed to focus on it for a moment. 'There's something hanging from underneath it,' he exclaimed. 'Quick, we've got to see it drop.'

The drone was quickly out of sight beyond the trees but they heard a change in the sound of its engine. It went higher and louder. 'I wonder if that change in the engine sound is because it's dropped its cargo,' said Mason.

'Like it's not having to work so hard,' added Harry.

Mason nodded. 'That would explain it.'

Then they heard the drone getting louder, coming towards them.

'Quick, hide, in case it's got a camera,' cried Charlie. 'We don't want to be spotted.'

They scuttled from the open meadow into the trees and lay in the grass. The drone passed overhead and then disappeared beyond the trees back the way it had come.

'So now we need to hunt for its cargo,' said Harry. 'What colour was the parachute?'

'Green, same as before,' replied Mason.

They hunted higher up the valley where the trees gave way to open meadow. From high up on the valley side they had a good view over Lucy's Wood and beyond. Finally, after half an hour of searching they gave up and collapsed onto the grass.

'Like looking for a needle in a haystack,' groaned Charlie. 'I thought it would be dead easy to find it.'

'Wait a minute,' said Mason, focusing his binoculars. 'Oh, it's just that fisherman, Sophya talked about. He's down along the edge of the river going back towards the village.'

'Has he got his beanie hat on?' asked Harry.

Mason nodded. 'Yes, but I can't see anything of his face.'

They filed back along the path, past the track which led up to the barn.

'At least sleeping in the den gives us a chance to hear it and be there when the drop happens,' said Charlie.

'If it happens again,' said Max.

'True,' agreed Charlie. 'Let's keep our fingers crossed.'

'Are we out on the water again today?' asked Max. 'Weather looks pretty good.'

'Yes we haven't paddled to the other side of the lake yet,' said Harry.

'And there's another island on the map we haven't explored called Lingy Holm,' said Mason.

'Right then, Lingy Holm, here we come,' said Max.

*

'So Miki the chef plays piano, then?' said Mason, later that morning. He was paddling slowly with Summer at the front of the paddle board. Harry was paddling the other board close beside them.

'He was very shy,' replied Summer. 'But he played this beautiful piece by someone called, er.. Rachimov.'

'Probably Rachmaninov,' suggested Harry.

'That was him,' said Summer.

'Sophya got a bit sad with the music and she was a bit angry when she found out Rachimov was a Russian.'

'Rachmaninov,' repeated Harry.

'Sorry,' said Summer.

'And Miki told you all this? I thought he couldn't speak much,' said Mason.

'He wrote it down, and no he doesn't speak much at all,' said Summer. 'But he has beautiful handwriting.'

There was a shout from across the water. 'Lingy Holm!' It was Max pointing to a rocky outcrop sticking up out of the water near the opposite shore. He was in the canoe with Charlie.

Mason waved to him. 'And I asked Thomas if farmers ever use drones to deliver stuff,' went on Mason.

'What did he say?' asked Harry.

'He said it's possible but he's never heard of it happening near the farm.'

As they paddled closer to the island they could see it was not the most exciting discovery. In fact there were two rock outcrops with a small

channel running between them. The larger island had a covering of short grass and bracken with a small tree crowning the highest point. The other outcrop was mainly bare rock with a couple of stunted bushes.

'So why didn't Sophya come this morning?' asked Harry.

'She was worried about the planes,' replied Summer. 'They really frighten her.'

Max had steered the canoe into the narrow channel between the two islands. He jumped out onto the small beach of the larger island and scrambled up to the top. He waved.

'Max should have brought a flag to plant on the top,' said Mason. 'He likes the idea of conquering islands.'

'Look there,' squealed Summer. 'Something moving, something furry. Is it a rat?'

'Where?' said Charlie.

'By that rock, next to those reeds. There it is again. I hope it isn't a rat. I'm not going on the island if it is.'

Charlie moved slowly towards the reeds. He crouched down. 'It's a baby rabbit. I think it's injured its leg.'

Summer was up and jumping off the paddleboard. She ran across the beach and crouched down next to Charlie. 'Let me see. Oh poor baby.'

'It can't really move much. One of its back legs has blood on it. Looks as if it's been attacked by something.'

'How did it get here?' asked Summer.

'Maybe it was being chased and decided to swim for it,' suggested Charlie.

'Rabbits can't swim, can they?'

Charlie nodded. 'Our next door neighbour has a pet rabbit and gets it swimming in their paddling pool.'

Summer smiled as she reached out and touched the soft fur of the rabbit. 'Aw, little baby, we need to take you home and get your leg mended. We can't leave you here.'

'Yes I think the crows and buzzards would have him for breakfast in no time,' said Charlie. 'Have we got anything to wrap him in?'

'Use my towel,' offered Max. 'It's in the canoe. Summer can hold him while we paddle back.'

'Oh, can I? Thanks Max.'

Summer laid out Max's towel and Charlie carefully lifted the baby rabbit and folded the towel over it so that just its head was peaking out.

Summer cuddled her precious bundle. 'C'mon little baby, we're going to make you better.'

'You go in the canoe, Summer, and I'll go on the paddle board. It'll be easier that way,' suggested Max.

'Thanks, Max. Yes, this is better.' Summer settled down in the bottom of the canoe holding the little rabbit close to her chest. 'We'll be just fine, won't we, bunny.'

The boys briefly scoured Lingy Holm but there was little of real interest.

'It would be good if we could camp at Lucy's Wood,' said Mason, 'and be there when the drone arrives.'

Harry shook his head. 'Are you still droning on about that drone? It was probably some nerd trying out his new toy. Probably won't happen again.'

'But there was the parachute and it was bigger than a toy that you'd buy in a toy shop. That drone was serious tech,' said Mason.

Harry yawned. 'If you say so.' He stretched and then clapped his hands together. 'I think we need a snack before we paddle back.'

They had packed drinks, sandwiches and slices of cake in backpacks which were lodged in the rear of the canoe. Charlie fetched them and everything was shared out. The boys sat on the rocks while Summer stayed in the canoe.

Harry was scanning the sky. He spotted a bird of prey wheeling high above Gowbarrow. 'Look up there. A buzzard's being buzzed by some other smaller birds.'

'They're very brave to take on a bird that size,' commented Max

'But they know what buzzards can do to their young,' added Harry. 'A buzzard would make mincemeat out of Summer's rabbit.'

Summer frowned at Harry. 'Don't say things like 'mincemeat', that's horrible.' She turned to her new pet. 'Don't worry bunny, no nasty buzzard is going to get anywhere near you while I'm here!'

*

Later that afternoon, when they arrived back at the farm, Summer and Charlie took the injured rabbit to the farmhouse. Summer was sure Victoria would know what to do.

'What have you got there?' asked Victoria.

Summer showed her what was inside the bundle.

'Oh, hallo little fella. What have you been up to?' She handled the rabbit carefully and inspected its injured leg. 'Something's been after you, hasn't it,' she murmured, as she gently felt along the leg and looked closely at the bloodied fur. 'Nothing broken, just a clean up job, I think, and a bandage for a few days.' She turned to Summer. 'And he'll need some careful nursing, of course.'

Summer smiled and nodded. 'Of course.'

'D'you ever hear drones going over the farm?' asked Charlie.

'Drones?' Victoria frowned.

'The last couple of mornings a drone has gone over the farm and up the valley and then come back and disappeared from where it came.'

'I think some of the hill farmers might be experimenting with using drones for mapping or checking on their stocks in the higher fells. I saw something on *Countryfile* the other day,' replied Victoria.

Charlie nodded. 'Could be. I suppose.'

'Do you know,' said Summer, 'the new chef, Miki at the hotel, plays the piano. Sophya and I caught him out, early in the morning when he didn't think anyone could hear. He's a bit shy but he plays really well.'

'How interesting,' said Victoria. 'A musical chef. That's something new.'

# CHAPTER 11

The weather was fine enough for the boys to sleep in the den again. Summer didn't want to leave the baby rabbit which she was keeping in a small cage that Victoria had found for her, so she slept in her normal bed in the cottage.

'Y'know, it's not likely someone is going to fly a drone three mornings in a row, is it?' said Harry.

'Might be,' replied Charlie. 'Victoria said the farmers might be using drones for mapping or checking on their sheep on the higher fells.'

'Oh, I never thought of that.'

'If I hear the sound of that drone I'm going to be out of here like an F-16. I'll beat all of you up that valley,' said Max. 'I want to see where that parachute lands.'

Mason was watching the glow of the moon rising. The sky was clear and there was no wind. There would be a good display of stars tonight. 'Why would farmers mapping the land or checking on their sheep be dropping things by parachute,' he mused. 'Doesn't make sense to me.'

'Let's get some sleep, just in case we have to dash up the valley like a flight of F-16s,' joked Harry.

'You wait,' said Max. 'You just wait and see.'

The night was still. Just the sound of owls calling in the woods and now and then the distant bark of a fox. The moonlight was bright casting shadows down the open hillside. Just before dawn a figure crossed the bridge in the village and headed up the lane. He checked his watch and pulled his hat lower over his head.

In the den Max was restless, something had nudged him awake. He looked at his watch - 4.30 a.m. Then he heard it. Far off. That insect-like whine. He was up and stumbling over the legs of the others.

'What's happening?' murmured Charlie.

'Drone,' hissed Max and he was off, out of the den and racing up the hillside to the path which led to the valley.

Charlie nudged the others awake and they crawled from the den. They were all feeling sleepy and sluggish. Max, however, was wide awake, and nearing the gate which led down across the meadow, through the trees and up the valley to Lucy's Wood. He could hear the sound of the drone getting closer but he was still ahead of it. He raced past the river cliff, out of the trees just as the drone passed overhead. Beneath it swung a parachute.

Max raced along the path which bordered Lucy's Wood, all the time trying to keep an eye on the drone which now hovered not far away. He stopped running and listened. He could hear a voice further down the hillside. Quietly he slithered down through the grass towards the river. He realised he was near that strange spiral of stones. He could hear the voice more clearly now and he could see a man standing. He was wearing a dark jacket and a beanie hat and speaking into a phone in a language Max didn't understand, a language which was hard and rough sounding.

The drone continued to hover and then the sound of the engine changed as a small parachute was released. Beneath it there was a small box-shaped object. It swung gently down to the ground and the man went forward and picked it up. He said a few words into his phone as the drone rose into the air and its engine picked up speed. Max watched its progress as it moved high enough to get above the trees. Then he turned around to where the man had been. But there was no-one there. He scanned along the valley bottom, but there was no sign of the man.

He heard the sound of running feet and the others arrived breathing hard and gasping to get their breath back.

'What did you see?' panted Mason.

'Was there a parachute?' asked Charlie.

Max nodded. 'There was a man waiting for it. He collected what was attached to the parachute and then I lost sight of him.'

'What was he wearing?' asked Harry.

'Dark jacket, beanie hat and he was foreign. I heard him speaking into a phone in this really hard-sounding language.'

'Bet he was the fisherman that Sophya saw the other morning.'

'Yes, he was carrying a long stick thing. Maybe it was a fishing rod.'

Mason put his hand on Max's shoulder. 'Well done little brother. You said you would do it and you did.'

'Yeah, well done, Max,' added Harry.

'So did you get here ahead of the drone,' asked Charlie.

Max nodded.

'Just like an F-16. Well done coz,' smiled Charlie.


Sophya opened her eyes wide. The drones again in her dreams? But no, this was real. She could hear an engine, far off, going away. She knew immediately what it was; it wasn't going up the valley but away towards the hill they called Gowbarrow. The sound got more faint by the minute until it was gone. She got out of bed and went to the window for some air.

There was movement below on the lane. It was the fisherman again. He wasn't going away this time but coming towards the hotel. She heard his boots on the gravel below. She looked down as he approached the staff entrance. Just before he opened the door he took off his beanie hat. She was surprised when she saw who it was - Miki ! She didn't know he was a fisherman. There was a lot she didn't know about him. First the piano playing, now Miki the fisherman. What more was there to know? she wondered.

Later that morning she went down to the farm to see how Summer's baby rabbit was doing. She saw Summer and the boys on the hillside next to the den.

'Hi,' she said. 'I've solved a mystery.'

'So have we,' said Mason. 'What's your mystery?'

'The fisherman, the one you call Beanie Man, guess who he is?'

'Go on, tell us,' urged Charlie.

'It's Miki, I saw him this morning coming back into the hotel with his fishing rod and his beanie hat.'

'It can't be,' said Max.

Sophya frowned. 'What do you mean?'

'I saw the fisherman this morning just below Lucy's Wood. There was another drone and a parachute dropping a box. He collected it.'

'I don't understand,' said Sophya. 'Why would Miki be collecting something dropped from a drone?'

'There can't be two men dressed like fishermen lurking about in the early hours,' said Harry.

'But the thing is, this man was speaking on a phone. And he had a weird foreign accent,' explained Max.

'What do you mean 'weird'?' asked Sophya.

'Like he was talking out of his throat, very rough and harsh.'

'But we know Miki has a speech problem,' said Charlie.

Mason shook his head. 'Do we, though? Does he really have a speech problem?'

'You mean he's been faking it all this time?' said Harry.

Mason shrugged. 'Seems like there's a lot we don't know.'

Sophya was staring past them. She didn't speak for a moment. Then she held up her two hands. 'I do not want you to say anything to anyone until I tell you. It is up to me to find out the truth about Miki or should I say Mikolaj. Promise me you will not say a word.'

They all nodded.

'So you do not know what it was that the drone dropped this morning?'

'Just a small box about ten centimetres square,' said Max.

Sophya was thoughtful for moment. 'Okay, now pretend nothing unusual has happened.' She looked at Summer. 'Do you understand Summer, not to say anything.'

Summer nodded. 'I understand.'

'So now I have to do some thinking,' said Sophya, and with that she walked off in the direction of the hotel.

The others watched her go and then looked at each other.

'Something really odd is going on,' commented Charlie, 'and we need to find out what it is.'

'But we can't do anything or say anything until Sophya's found out more about Miki,' added Mason.

'We could go up to Lucy's Wood and have another look around. See if there are any clues,' suggested Harry.

Max was frowning. 'I've been thinking. You know I said that where the drone made the drop was near that pattern of stones like a spiral?'

'Go on,' said Mason.

'Well maybe they use that spiral as the target for the drop. A camera on the drone could pick that up quite easily.'

Harry nodded. 'Hey, good thinking, Max,'

'I need to go and check on my bunny,' said Summer, 'so I'll stay here.'

'Okay. So that's the plan for the morning. Go and check out the stone spiral, see what we can find?' said Mason.

'Agreed,' nodded Charlie. 'Let's get sorted. Meet here in half an hour.'

*

By the time Sophya reached the hotel she had worked out what she had to do. Before going up to her room she stood at the bottom of the fire escape and looked up at the windows. She was working out which window was Miki's room. She counted along and tried to remember the sequence of rooms on the corridor. Miki's was two doors down. She looked again. Below his room was the sloping roof of the laundry. There was a water butt against the wall which she could stand on to get on the roof. The question was could she get his window open?

However, it couldn't happen right now. She had to check the rota to see when he would be working in the kitchen. She went in the staff entrance and met her mother. Immediately, she knew something was wrong. Her mother's eyes were red. She had been crying.

'What is the matter, mama?'

Her mother shook her head and put a handkerchief to her eyes. She sat down heavily on the chair. 'I had a message from your baba. She is still in Kherson and she is okay but she thinks your papa has been taken prisoner.'

'Oh mama, no,' cried Sophya. 'How I hate those Russians! And we can do nothing!'

'They sometimes do prisoner exchanges,' said her mother. 'That is what we must pray for.'

'Oh, papa, papa, I pray that they do not hurt you.' She looked again at her mother. 'You need help today mama. Is Miki in the kitchen? Is he there to help you?'

Her mother nodded. 'Yes we finish at two. When the lunches are over.'

That was the information Sophya needed. 'I'm going to my room. I must write a message to baba. I will see you later.'

She looked at her watch. She had an hour.

*

The boys made their way up the valley. At the stone sign by the wall they cut down to the river away from Lucy's Wood. They passed the pillar with the brass bell, went through the gate and up to the flat area where the spiral of stones was located.

Mason nodded. 'You're right, Max, from the air this would be a good target for a camera on a drone to pick up.'

Max was already going round the spiral to the central

stone, eyes scanning the ground. Harry had gone further away into some trees and Charlie worked his way along the river bank. The river was running quite fast and there were some deep plunge pools so he had to be careful. But then he spotted something hanging close to the water. It was another parachute!

'Hey, over here,' he shouted.

He had to wade into the river to reach it but submerged below the parachute was a small rectangular box. He lifted it dripping from the water. It was fairly heavy and wrapped thickly with black plastic tape. There were no markings on the outside.

The others quickly joined him. 'How about this, then,' said Charlie, holding up his trophy.

'Great work,' said Max, 'anyone got a knife?'

'Here,' said Mason, 'I knew my Swiss army knife would come in useful sometime.' He handed the knife to Charlie.

Charlie sliced carefully along one edge of the box. He did the same along another two sides. Then he was able to lift the lid of the box. Inside was something weighty wrapped in a black plastic bag. He sliced through the side of the bag and took out a solid roll of paper.

Charlie removed a rubber band which held the paper together .

'It's a roll of money!' exclaimed Mason.

'Twenties and tens!' cried Charlie thumbing through the notes. 'There must be hundreds of pounds here!'

'Well spotted, Charlie,' said Max. 'Now we know.'

'But why is someone sending rolls of money to Miki?' asked Mason.

'That's what Sophya is trying to find out,' said Harry.

*

She was at the window trying to move the catch with a carving knife she'd taken from the kitchen. It had been easy to climb up on the laundry roof and get there. But Sophya had to work quickly. Finally the catch shifted and she was able to slide the window up enough to climb inside Miki's room.

She went first to the drawers. There were just clothes and pairs of socks, shirts hanging in a wardrobe, Miki's white chef's overall on a hanger.

Then she stooped down and looked under the bed. There was a leather satchel bag with two straps. She undid the straps and felt inside. She pulled out packets of papers. Inside one envelope were photographs. First, Miki and a young woman. On the back was the date '2019' and the names *Olga* and *Ivan.* She recognised the domes of Red Square in Moscow, the Russian capital. Another showed a younger Miki with his arms round two older people. On the back the names *Ivan, Dmitri* and *Svetlana* and the location *St. Petersburg 2016*. But these were

Russian cities. And so was Miki's real name Ivan?

Sophya was puzzled. She glanced round the room and her eyes spotted something intriguing. Next to the bed was a waste paper basket. There were pieces of a torn photograph among some scrunched up tissues. She picked out the pieces and laid them out on the carpet. As she fitted them together, her pulse started racing. Here was an older 'Ivan' wearing a soldier's uniform with that horrific 'Z' sign on his sleeve. He was standing with three other soldiers next to an armoured troop carrier. The other three were smiling but Ivan looked very serious. On the back the words *Belarus 2022*.

Belarus, the country which bordered Ukraine in the north and from where Putin's invasion had started.

Sophya sank back on her heels. Her heart was beating fast. Her forehead was sweating. So Miki was really Ivan, a Russian soldier! That's why he had pretended he couldn't speak so that he wouldn't get found out. What was he doing here? Was he following Sophya and her mother? Was he intending to kill them? Was he a spy?

The thoughts pounded in her head, fingers of fear scurried up and down her spine. And suddenly the bedroom door was opening and there was Miki looking shocked, mouth open.

Quickly, Sophya picked up the knife and held it towards Miki. 'Stay there,' she hissed. 'It's Ivan isn't it! And you are Russian, not Polish.

And you can speak, can't you? Go on speak, Ivan, say something. Tell me why you are here. Are you going to kill me and kill my mother? Go on, are you!'

'Please, please, you do not understand,' he murmured.

'Oh I do,' cried Sophya, 'I know exactly what you Russians do. You are trained to kill, to stamp on people who are not Russian. You have tried to destroy my country.'

Ivan held his open palms towards Sophya. 'Please listen,' he said and took a step forward.

'Get back,' cried Sophya and she thrust the knife forward towards him. 'You're not going to get me.' She backed towards the open window and quickly jumped out onto the roof of the laundry. In seconds she was down on the ground and running for her life.

# CHAPTER 12

The first spots of rain began falling just before tea time. Heavy grey clouds were sagging over Gowbarrow Fell.

Charlie was by the window. 'That sounded like thunder.'

The boys were in the lounge which looked down the valley to the east. They were hoping to hear from Sophya. They had said nothing to the adults about what they knew about Miki, the drones and the money.

Max was restless to do something. 'Maybe we should go along to the hotel. Check out what's happening.'

There was a flash of lightning and then a few seconds later a distant growl of thunder. Then they heard footsteps and a knocking at the cottage door.

Harry opened it to see Sophya's mother, Anna, and Miki huddled under an umbrella.

'Come in out of the rain,' said Harry.

They stepped inside. Anna was clearly very agitated. Her voice wavered. 'Is Sophya here? I'm very worried about her.'

'No, she left us a couple of hours ago to go back to the hotel.'

'Sophya had an argument with Miki and ran off.'

Miki held up a hand to interrupt. 'I have something I must tell you.'

'So you can speak,' said Mason. 'I knew it.'

'My name is not Mikolaj it is Ivan Sidorov. I am not Polish. I am a deserter from the Russian army. I would not fight Putin's evil war so I escaped before I could be sent to fight.'

'How did you get here?' asked Max.

'It is a long story. I will tell you one day. But Sophya is frightened of me. That is why she ran away when she found out I was Russian.'

'How did she find out?' asked Charlie.

'Too many questions,' said Anna. 'The important thing is to find her. She will be frightened and the noise of this storm will bring back memories of the war, I know it.'

By now the adults had heard the commotion and were listening in. 'We've only got a couple of hours of daylight left,' said Mason's father. 'Any ideas where Sophya might go to hide?'

'Maybe Lucy's Barn?' suggested Max.

'But wait a minute,' interrupted Harry. 'D'you remember when we went to the first island, Sophya said that it would be good place to escape to if ever she needed to.'

'Yes, I thought it was a weird thing to say at the time,' nodded Mason, 'but you're right. Maybe she would feel safe there. And there are always canoes and paddle boards left down on that beach.'

'It's a long way for her to go.'

'People will do anything when they're desperate,' said Mason's father. 'I'll drive us down. Get the life jackets and bring paddles. And be quick.'

Summer's mother turned to Anna. 'Let's get you warm and dry. I'll make some tea, and maybe you can tell us more about yourself, Miki, or should I say, Ivan.'

It was only a short drive down to the beach at Glencoyne Bay. The wind was whipping up waves on the surface of the lake.

'This could be tricky,' commented Charlie. 'There's quite a wind blowing.'

Harry's father made a quick decision. 'We'll borrow these two canoes. They'll be safer than the paddleboards.'

On a bright sunny day the distance out to Norfolk Island had been a pleasant, easy paddle. On this grey, stormy afternoon the distance looked more challenging. They pulled hard on their paddles to get started then got into a smoother rhythm to increase speed. The wind was in their faces and, now and then, people behind got peppered with spray from the person at the front.

'Steady on, Max,' said Harry's dad, 'I'm getting soaked here.'

In the other canoe, Charlie was at the front, Mason's father in the middle and Mason at the back. Mason was trying to focus on the island with his binoculars. 'I see something,' he shouted. 'There's a paddle board pulled up under the trees.'

'We always said it might make a good place to camp,' added Harry.

'Sophya must have remembered,' said Mason.

'It might not be her,' warned Mason's father. 'Could be someone else doing a quick overnight.'

There were large rocks to navigate round before they could pull up on the small beach. Harry was out of the canoe and up the rock face first, clambering to get to the top. Max quickly followed behind him.

When they looked down from the top of the rocky peak they saw an orange tent on the narrow ledge below them. Harry waved to the others to be quiet, putting his hand to his lips. 'I think it could be her,' he whispered to Max.

Max slithered down the slope above the tent, missed his footing and fell in a heap by the door of the tent. The door was unzipped and a bearded face looked at him. 'What the heck are you doing?' grunted the man.

'We're looking for a young girl,' replied Harry. 'She's run away. We thought she might have come here.'

'What does she look like?'

'She often wears a baseball cap, has blonde hair, and she's about my height,' said Harry. 'She's called Sophya.'

The man nodded. 'I'll look out for her.'

'Sorry to disturb you,' called Mason's father.

'It was a bit of a shock.'

'Yes, sorry,' said Max.

They reassembled down on the beach.

'So, any ideas, boys?' asked Harry's father. 'It's going to be dark soon.'

'I think we should try Lucy's Barn,' suggested Charlie.

'Well, let's get back first and get warmed up. We'll need head torches if we're going up to the woods.'

They set off across the lake. Luckily the wind was behind them and it was not long before they were on the beach at Glencoyne.

Back at the cottages, they warmed up with mugs of hot chocolate. When they mentioned going to check Lucy's Barn, Summer was not sure. 'But that's where she cried. It made her sad.'

'But she knows it, and it's warm and dry,' explained Max.

'I must come too,' insisted Ivan. 'It was I who made her run away.'

'Okay, get the rain gear and head torches,' said Mason's father.

'There's a survival kit in the cupboard,' suggested Harry, 'with a foil blanket. I'll bring that.'

Summer was keen not to be left out. 'I want to come too. Sophya's my special friend, remember.'

'Get your waterproofs on then,' ordered Mason. 'And be quick.'

They assembled in the courtyard, the children, Ivan and the two dads.

'I'll lead, I know the way,' said Max.

Harry tapped Max on the shoulder. 'Don't go so fast this time.'

'Okay,' replied Max. 'Are we ready?'

In single file they made their way up the field to the gate and the path which led to the valley and Lucy's Wood. They nudged past a flock of sheep who were sheltering near the field wall. The thunder still growled but in the past half hour they had seen no lightning. The rain blew in sharp gusts which stung their faces and trickled down their necks.

'Yuk, this rain's a pain,' said Charlie.

'Yes, my feet are soaking, I should've worn wellies,' moaned Harry.

'Wellies are no good,' said Mason. 'Give you blisters.'

'Well at least they'd be dry blisters not wet ones!'

Max stopped at the gate by the lane and waited for the others to catch up. 'Are we all here?' he asked.

'Yes,' said Summer, 'I'm here.'

'Carry on, Max. Take it steady down along the riverside. There's a steep drop there. Watch your footing,' warned his father.

They could hear the Aira river far below, roaring through the gorge as they skirted the meander and headed up into the meadow to the gap in the wall and the stone sign for Lucy's Wood. Max waited again until Mason, who was bringing up the rear, had arrived.

'Okay,' called Mason, 'lead on.'

*

Sophya couldn't stop the shaking. She pulled her sleeping bag higher over her head. It wasn't so much the cold but the fear. She could hear the whirring of the drones, the whistle of the shells and then the explosions. She could taste the dust and hear the cries of injured people. And there was nothing she could do. She saw the shadows of Russian soldiers in the darkness, the points of their guns sihouetted, the sound of their boots on the gravel road outside her house. Would they break in, smash down the doors?

There was another roll of thunder, then a flash of lightning and Sophya cried out, 'Papa, my papa, where are you?'

She had run and run from the Russian soldier, Ivan, or was he Miki? She was so confused that just along the corridor from where she had been sleeping was a Russian soldier who might have a gun or a knife. Who might be planning to hurt and kill them. Had he followed them there? What was he up to? Why had he hidden who he really was? Why had he tricked them all?

She had run with the sound of thunder in her ears, with flashes of lightning blinding her eyes. She had tripped several times, falling into mud, sodden grass and leaves. Her face was smeared with dirt and her legs were soaking wet. The sky had darkened and then the shapes of the trees were like so many soldiers' rifles with their deadly bayonets. The thunder was as if

missiles were exploding all around. She saw again the smoke and felt the ground shaking, buildings crashing into mountains of rubble and dust. Her body continued its shaking, her teeth chattering, her arms and legs shivering. 'Papa, where are you?' she cried out again.

*

Max found the path which led the way up to the barn. He waited for them to catch up.

'It's darker up here through the trees. Watch your step,' he warned. 'Not far now.'

The stream which ran down the hillside was now a torrent. The branches of the pine trees behind the barn whipped the air. Max waited at the barn door for the others to arrive. His father went forward and opened the door.

It was dry inside. The candle in the lantern in the centre of room glowed warmly. The sound of the wind was left outside as they trooped in quietly, their eyes adjusting to the gloom.

Summer looked around. 'She's not here. Oh, where can she be!'

'I was so sure she'd be here,' said Charlie. 'She liked this place even if it made her feel sad.'

Mason shone his torch into all the corners of the room but it looked much the same as when they visited the previous time. No-one had been there since their last visit.

Max held up his hand. 'Wait a minute. I just remembered something.'

'Go on,' said Harry.

'D'you remember I told you about a little hut I found up in the woods, a one person house?'

'And I asked, if it was full of little people,' added Mason.

Max nodded. 'Well, there was a platform that this little hut stood on and underneath I remember seeing a backpack with a blue and yellow ribbon attached, you know, the Ukrainian colours. I thought it had been left by people who used it for an overnight stay.'

'And you think it could be Sophya's,' asked Summer, 'with that ribbon on?'

Max shrugged. 'It's worth a look.'

'Can you remember the way?' asked Charlie.

'It was a path up behind the barn, through the trees. There were coloured marks on posts. I followed the red markers.'

Charlie was first out of the barn and using his head torch to find the path he saw the first red marker. 'This way,' he said. 'Careful of the tree roots, it's a bit knobbly.'

Max was close behind him. 'I think the path bends to the right. Yes, see that marker.'

Charlie raced on along the path. Ahead the beam of his torch suddenly picked up the flat side of a wooden structure and the pitched roof of a small hut.

'The door's round the back,' called out Max.

'So this is your little house,' said Harry. 'We didn't believe you.'

'I know, but this is where I saw the backpack with the ribbon.'

There was a flash of lightning across the valley as the others arrived and then, very close, a crash of thunder. From inside the hut came a cry of 'No! No! Please no!'

'That's Sophya's voice,' whispered Summer.

Max's father went forward and opened the door. He shone his torch inside. Two staring eyes looked back at him, eyes full of terror. 'No, no!' cried Sophya.

Summer knelt down beside her friend. 'It's me, Summer, it's going to be okay, Sophya. You're safe now.'

*

Later that evening, after Sophya had been safely tucked up in her bed at the hotel, and a tearful Anna had hugged everyone, including Ivan, the children returned to the cottages for burgers and hot dogs.

'So what have you found out about Ivan?' asked Charlie's mother.

'I was walking with him and asked him what his job had been before the war,' replied Mason. 'He said he was a chef in a big hotel in Moscow....'

'And he was a concert pianist,' added Charlie.

'And he did some cookery training in a hotel in London when he was nineteen,' put in Harry.

His mother nodded. 'He says that he lives in fear that the Russian secret police will try to find him.'

'Is that why he ran away when we caught him playing the piano?' asked Summer.

'Probably. He doesn't want to draw attention to himself.'

'So why did he pretend not to be able to speak?' asked Mason.

'Maybe thought people would hear his Russian accent,' suggested Harry, 'and his cover would be blown.'

'He said he was terrified when he got the letter at his home, that he had to join the army,' said Max. 'And when he went for army training he knew he couldn't do it, couldn't hold a gun and pull the trigger.'

Mason nodded. 'His words were: I use my hands for creating beautiful things, wonderful food, beautiful music, not for killing people.'

'Poor fellow,' said his father. 'He was in tears when we found Sophya. He was so relieved.'

'What about the drones dropping money? What was that all about?' asked Charlie.

'Seems, it's to help him survive the war. There's a network of people in England, some are Russian who hate Putin, others are just lovers of Ivan's piano playing who know of him and know it's dangerous for him to open a bank account or to use his mobile phone too much. So they try to get money to him in any way they can that's safe. In the north of England they're trying out using drones,' explained his father.

'War's a horrible thing,' said Max, 'and Ivan must be always looking over his shoulder.'

'But, anyway, he wants to put on a party for us all, to thank us for being kind to him.'

'Will he make more Polish food with flags on?' asked Summer.

'I don't think he needs to stick to Polish food. That was just another way of trying to keep his true identity a secret,' said her father.

'Maybe he'll do Russian food now.'

'We'll have to wait and see,' said Charlie's mother. 'Anyway, you lot, it's time for bed. Let's get moving.'

'Auntie Katie, can I see Sophya in the morning,' asked Summer. 'She hasn't seen Pixie, my bunny.'

'We'll have to see how she is. Now off to bed young lady. You've had a busy day.'

# CHAPTER 13

Sophya had slept the whole of the following morning. By the afternoon she was keen to see the others, to find out what had been happening.

Summer was kneeling down by the rabbit hutch when Sophya arrived. 'Hey, I missed you,' grinned Summer, jumping up and hugging her friend.

'I missed you all,' replied Sophya. She held out a piece of carrot. A furry nose nuzzled at it and then the baby rabbit took the carrot and started chewing.

'See, she likes you.'

Sophya nodded. 'I think she likes the carrot. When will you let her go free?'

'When Victoria says her leg is better. But I don't really want to.'

Sophya shook her head. 'You can't keep a wild rabbit in a cage. It's like a prison.'

'Did you say your daddy is in a prison?'

'Yes. The only good thing is, we know he's still alive. He could have been killed. But he's somewhere safe away from the bombs and the fighting. So that's a good thing.'

'Have you seen Ivan?'

'He came with my mother to my room and he cried. I've never seen a man cry before. He said he was so sorry about everything; about frightening me, about the war, about my papa.'

'Did you know he was a chef before the war and a concert pianist. He said he wouldn't hold a gun and so he ran away from the army.'

'So not every Russian is a bad Russian,' said Sophya.

'I think Ivan is a good Russian,' agreed Summer. 'And he's going to do a concert and do some nice food for us all.'

Sophya smiled. 'I think I'm ready for some nice food. I hope Ivan plays that music again, you know that one he played before.'

'I'm sure he will. Was it by Rachimov?'

'Something like that,' replied Sophya.


The children helped to sweep out the old ballroom, put up banners and Ukrainian ribbons. The adults shifted furniture, bringing chairs from a storeroom and setting up a long table.

Anna called over to Harry and Mason. 'Please, boys, I have a flag I would like you to hang somewhere. I always carry it with me.'

They unfolded a large Ukrainian flag.

'How about behind the piano?' suggested Harry.

Anna nodded. 'Perfect,' she said.

Charlie and Max raised the lid of the grand piano and then couldn't resist tapping the keys to see the hammers striking the strings.

'It needs dusting and polishing,' said Max's mother. 'Here you are,' she said handing them dusters and a sprayer.

'Do we have to?' groaned Charlie.

'You've got to earn your supper.'

118

Sophya and Summer were outside collecting flowers which they put in a vase and placed on a table at the side of the piano.

Charlie's father set up some music speakers and a music player and by early afternoon, after the hotel lunches had been served, they were ready for the party.

Ivan and Anna had spent much of the morning preparing food - a mixture of Russian, Ukrainian and English. It was carried in from the kitchen by two of the hotel staff. By the time the last plate was brought in, the table was almost sagging with a colourful array of meats, pastries, cakes and desserts.

'Wow, what a feast!' said Harry.

Mason's father tapped a glass with a spoon. 'Take your places folks. Let's get this party started.'

Anna and Ivan were the last to come in and sit down. They received a round of applause and Ivan bowed and put his hand to his heart and looked very emotional. He forced a smile and gestured to everyone with his hands together like in a prayer.

Summer was watching him. 'I think Ivan's a bit sad.'

'Maybe he misses his home and his family,' suggested Sophya.

'I think so.'

Harry had put on some Ed Sheeran music for the meal but when they had finished eating Anna called him over. She whispered to him and gave him her phone which had some special music stored on it. He took it across to his father who picked up a glass and tapped it three times. Everyone looked towards him and stopped talking.

'Anna wants you to hear some Ukrainian music,' he said. 'She's going to show us a dance and she wants us all to have a go at doing it. Okay?'

Anna got up and stood in the middle of the dance floor. She closed her eyes and waited for the music.

It was a single voice, a very powerful man's voice rising and falling carrying a haunting folk song and accompanied by a strong clapping beat. Anna started moving her feet and clapping her hands and nodding to everyone to join the clapping. After a few moments of showing the dance steps she went across to Ivan, took his hand and pulled him onto the dance floor alongside her. He was shy and reluctant at first but then he started copying Anna's movements, holding her hand and turning slowly to the rhythm of the song.

Sophya watched her mother, watched her dancing with this young Russian, this man she had feared and run away from. She saw her mother lost in the music and the dance and it made her feel so happy.

Harry's parents got up and joined them and nodded to the others to get up too. Soon the ballroom was alive with movement, with the sound of clapping, bodies turning and feet tapping the floor to the rhythm of the song.

'Am I a cool dancer or what,' grinned Harry.

'Not bad,' replied his mother. 'Here, give me a twirl,' and she took his hand.

He tried to pull back, saying, 'Ugh, too embarrassing,' but she held on to his hand and pushed him round in a circle.

Sophya moved among the boys taking each of their hands in turn, spinning round and moving on. She had done this dance many times before.

When the song finished everyone clapped and went back to their seats. That is, except Ivan, who bowed to Anna and went across to the piano and sat down.

Before he started he turned, waited for a moment and then said, 'I hope I can show you that not everything that comes out of Russia is monstrous and threatening. That there is beauty, gentleness and romance. I am going to play a small section of a piece by the great Russian composer Rachmaninov. Like me, he fled from Russia, not during a war but during the revolution of 1917. He wrote this in Switzerland in 1934. It's called *Rhapsody on a theme of Paganini*. I hope you enjoy it.'

The music started slowly with a simple theme which flowed from Ivan's fingers and filled the ballroom. It rang in the high dusty corners of the ceiling, it rolled along the walls with their faded wallpaper, it filled the empty spaces of the room and gradually the theme built up to a surging wave of sound which finally quietened and fell to a gentle ending.

For a moment there was silence in the room. Then Sophya started clapping, she had tears on her face and was shaking her head. Then she was up, out of her seat and running across to Ivan and hugging him. He was startled at first but then put his arms round her and held her.

The clapping continued. Sophya pulled away, looked briefly at Ivan, wiped her eyes and whispered, 'Thank you,' and returned to her seat. Ivan got up, turned and bowed and clapped back in thanks.

'Wow,' exclaimed Max, 'that was amazing.'

'I'd like to play like that one day,' said Mason.

'Yes, it was brilliant,' added Harry.

'Not like your dancing,' teased Charlie. 'That needs working on.'

'You can talk. You've got two left feet.'

Summer wagged her finger. 'Stop scoring points, you two.'

'Yes,' added Sophya, 'let's get some real dancing going and see what you can do. I'm changing the music.'

From then on it was modern music starting with Dua Lipa, one of Sophya's favourites. The boys cavorted around, Charlie played his air guitar, his father did some typical 'dad dancing' which Harry said was 'really embarrassing' and finally they all stood in a line and followed some line dancing moves that were led by one of the waitresses.

Hot, tired and thirsty they finally flopped down. It had been a memorable day.

'Will you come with us and climb Gowbarrow Fell tomorrow?' Harry asked Sophya.

'Yes, we're going to let Pixie go free,' added Summer. 'Victoria says her leg's better and she's ready.'

Sophya nodded. 'As long as you warn me about any planes you hear coming.'

'We will,' nodded Mason, 'don't worry.'

'I will look forward to it then,' replied Sophya.

# CHAPTER 14

They decided to release the rabbit at the foot of Gowbarrow, rather than carrying the cage up the hill.

Summer cuddled her little furry bundle for one last time. 'I'm going to miss you, little Pixie,' she said and nuzzled her nose into the baby rabbit's soft fur.

'I will miss you, too,' said Sophya, putting her arm round Summer's shoulders. 'Maybe you will come to my country and visit when the war is over. You will love Odesa. It is one of the best places in the world.'

'How long will that be,' asked Harry, 'until the war is over?'

Sophya shook her head. 'I don't know but I hope it will end soon.' Then her face lit up. 'And there was some good news - we heard from my grandmother that my father is to be released in a prisoner exchange. He will be able to go home for a time. He must get his strength back. My grandmother will feed him her special chicken and vegetable soup, which he loves.'

'That's great news,' agreed Charlie. 'And how is Ivan?'

Sophya smiled. 'Ah, Ivan - he is like a little boy, very happy. He received a large parcel this morning and is very excited about it. He showed it to me.'

'What was it,' asked Harry, 'inside the parcel?'

'I am not allowed to tell you. He wants it to be a surprise.'

'I'm glad he's happier,' said Mason.

'He is much happier now that he can be himself and not pretend that he is Polish and unable to speak.' Sophya clapped her hands and smiled. 'And do you know, he is going to help me with playing the piano again. He wants us to learn a duet.'

'A Russian, Ukrainian duo, playing the piano together - wow, that will be something special,' commented Charlie.

'Exactly,' added Sophya. 'We want to show that there is hope for the future.'

Summer put down the little rabbit in a clump of grass near the edge of a small coppice of hazel and beech trees. Charlie's father said it would be a good place for the rabbit to find nuts and forage for other food. The rabbit hesitated for a moment and then hopped a couple of times before scurrying further into the woodland showing its little white bobtail for the last time.

'Don't be sad,' said Sophya. 'Rabbits are wild, they want to be free. You have saved him, helped him get better and now it's time he went his own way.'

'I know,' replied Summer sadly. 'I know.'

They made their way up the side of the fell on a path which wound through the heather and bracken. Finally they could see the sun glinting on the surface of the lake below them.

'It's like a scarf of silk thrown down across

the mountains,' commented Sophya. 'So beautiful.'

'Do you have lakes and mountains in Ukraine?' asked Mason.

'In the Carpathian Mountains we have many beautiful rivers and lakes just like this.'

There was a distant engine noise. 'Plane incoming,' shouted Max. 'Just a trainer I think, not a fighter. But it's still noisy. Yes it's a T-38.'

The small jet plane sped towards them, low down in the valley. Sophya put her hands over her ears and crouched down.

'Group hug,' shouted Harry and all four boys and Summer formed a huddle around her.

'Hang in there, Sophya, soon gone,' said Charlie.

The scream of the jet engine came and went quickly and faded away down the lake. Everyone came up for air.

'I'm okay,' nodded Sophya. 'Thanks for the huddle.'

They walked across the flat summit of Gowbarrow Fell and stopped at the mound of rocks which marked the highest point.

'Let's stop here for a moment,' suggested Sophya. 'I need for my heart to stop racing. And I want to take in this lovely view.'

Harry shared his bag of Haribo sweets as they watched the steamer chugging its way down the lake and a couple of sailboats tacking across its wake.

'Listen,' said Charlie. 'What's that?' He pointed to a whirring speck rising from down in the valley.

'It's a drone,' said Max.

'And it's heading this way,' added Mason.

Summer looked across at Sophya, concerned that she might be frightened. But she was strangely calm.

'It's got something dangling from it,' shouted Max.

'It's another of those parachutes with a box underneath,' exclaimed Harry.

'Maybe we've won the lottery and it's another bundle of money,' said Charlie.

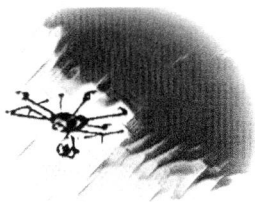

The drone, weird and insect-like, whirred over their heads and then hovered directly above them.

'Look out,' shouted Max, 'we could get bombed!'

There was a click and a change in the sound of the drone, as the parachute was released and started its descent with the box swaying in the wind. The drone continued to hover and then moved off back the way it had come.

There was a soft thud as the box and parachute landed. They ran across to it and stared at it for moment. Mason was quick to find his knife. 'Shall I open it?'

'Go on,' urged Max.

Mason cut carefully along the sides of the box and then lifted the top. Inside was a small package and a piece of paper. Harry opened the paper and read the words:

*To my new friends so you know there is at least one good Russian. Ivan xx*

'It's a little cake!' cried Mason. 'Ivan has sent us a cake.' He unwrapped the package to reveal a cake decorated with the flags of Ukraine and Great Britain.

Mason turned to Sophya. 'You knew, didn't you?'

Sophya smiled and nodded. 'He showed me the drone yesterday so I would not be frightened of it, but he did not say he was sending a cake.'

'With our two flags on it,' added Summer.

'And there's a little wooden knife,' said Harry. 'I think, Sophya, you should cut the cake.'

'I think I should,' she agreed. 'Thank you for being such great friends. I will never forget you.'

Printed in Great Britain
by Amazon